MURDER
AT FLOOD TIDE

*Detectives hunt a killer on Edinburgh's
streets*

ROBERT McNEILL

Published by The Book Folks

London, 2019

© Robert McNeill

ISBN 978-1-6943-0572-5

www.thebookfolks.com

This book is the second to feature DI Jack Knox. Look out for the first, THE INNOCENT AND THE DEAD, and the third, DEAD OF NIGHT, both available on Kindle and in paperback.

A list of characters featured in this book can be found at the back.

Chapter One

Soon after the barman had served him his pint, a young blonde at a nearby table glanced over and smiled. A mousy-looking brunette sitting beside her whispered something, then both women giggled.

He smiled back, thinking she looked like a woman he'd picked up in Doonan's a month earlier.

A bitch he'd come so very close to killing.

She had platinum hair, too – most likely from a bottle. Early twenties, slight build. Glossy lipstick painted on rosebud lips.

On leaving Doonan's she accepted his offer of a lift home, and on the way there he stopped in a cul-de-sac. They began necking, and a short time later moved to the back of his van.

She hitched up her skirt and he unbuckled his trousers, only to discover that he couldn't perform.

'What's the matter, darlin',' she asked with a hint of mockery, 'too much to drink?'

It was almost as if a switch had been flicked inside him: he seized her throat and began to compress her larynx. She quickly began struggling for breath, arms and legs flailing.

He moved his knees in an attempt to pinion her thighs, then her survival instinct took over: she clenched her fist and aimed a blow at his head.

Her punch caught the side of his mouth and he slackened his grip. She let out a scream, and seconds later a man's voice sounded at the other side of the street: 'Hey – you in the van! What's going on?'

He removed his hands from her neck and glanced out of the window, then she pressed her advantage. She gave him a shove, opened the door, and staggered outside.

'Help!' she cried, her voice now almost a croak. 'Someone's trying to kill me.'

It took only a moment for him to clamber into the driving seat, start the engine, and floor the accelerator.

He glanced at his watch as he joined the intersection and saw it was half past one. The cul-de-sac had been dimly lit and his lights switched off, so there was little chance the man had taken his number. He was equally confident the bitch hadn't seen it either.

The police would've been alerted, of course, but he knew the area and the twenty-minute drive home had proven uneventful.

Just to be safe, though, the next day he contacted a mate with a half share in a commercial vehicle dealership in Broxburn. He drove there the following Monday and traded his van for a more up-to-date model.

Suddenly a voice cut into his reverie, bringing him back to the present: 'Quiet tonight.'

The man who had spoken was seated on a barstool to his right. He was in his mid- to late-twenties.

'Sorry?' he replied, not sure he'd heard correctly.

The man waved to their surroundings. 'I was saying it's quiet here for a Friday. Considering it's Festival time. Tourists and the like.'

He turned and gave the place a cursory glance. 'I wouldn't know. I'm not a regular.'

The man nodded. 'No, neither am I.' He jerked his thumb in the direction of the exit. 'After work I usually pop into the Greyfriars Bobby.' He raised his pint and took a long swallow, then replaced his glass on the bar.

'Couldn't wait till I got that far tonight, though. Temperature's given me quite a drouth.'

'You work near here?'

The man acknowledged this with a wave of his hand. 'Aye. I'm a storeman with Carson's Printers. In the Cowgate, just around the corner.'

He nodded acknowledgement, but said nothing.

'You're on your own then?'

He gave the man a quizzical look.

'What I mean is, you're not waiting for a girl?'

He shook his head. 'No, no girlfriend.'

The man leaned closer and lowered his voice. 'Reason for asking,' he said, 'there's a wee blonde at a table over there giving you the eye.'

He took a swig of his pint and returned the glass to the counter. 'So I've noticed.'

'Thing is, I quite fancy her pal. What do you say to chatting them up? I think we'd be in with a chance.'

He considered this for a moment, then picked up his glass. 'Okay. I'm game if you are.'

They walked over to the table where the women were seated, then he gestured to a couple of vacant chairs.

'Mind if we join you?'

The blonde looked up at him and smiled. 'I don't.' She glanced at the brunette. 'You, Shona?'

Shona gave a little giggle, then shrugged. 'Okay with me.'

As they took their seats, he said, 'My friend...' He hesitated, giving the storeman a questioning look.

'Joe,' the man said.

'Joe was just saying how quiet this place is for a Friday night. I told him I'm seldom in here.'

Shona nodded. 'It's usually busier, this time of year anyway.' She turned to the blonde. 'Don't you agree, Connie?'

Her friend glanced at her wristwatch. 'It's five to nine,' she said. 'The tattoo starts at nine o'clock. There were a few tourists here when we arrived. Quieter now they've left for the Castle.'

As she spoke, he appraised her features. She had an aquiline nose, blue eyes and unblemished skin. Up close, though, he saw dark roots at her hairline, confirming that, just like the woman he'd picked up at Doonan's, the colour wasn't natural.

'So,' Joe was saying. 'You know the Quaich. I take it you both work locally?'

Shona nodded. 'Yes, Standard & Municipal Insurance at West Port. We're in admin.'

As her friend spoke, Connie maintained eye contact, smiling coquettishly. It was obvious she fancied him.

He stood up then and indicated the bar. 'Okay, Connie, Shona,' he said, 'what'll you have to drink?'

'Vodka and tonic for me, please,' Shona said.

'Fine. Connie?'

'Daiquiri, please,' she said. Then, fluttering her eyelashes, she added, 'By the way, you haven't told us your name.'

'John,' he said. 'John Masters.' He nodded towards his new-found acquaintance. 'Joe?'

'Pint of lager, John, thanks.'

Chapter Two

Detective Inspector Jack Knox was buttering a slice of toast when his phone rang. He wiped his hands on a dish towel, retrieved the cordless unit from the kitchen table, and pressed *accept*.

'Knox,' he said.

'Morning, boss.'

Knox immediately recognised the voice of his partner, Detective Sergeant Bill Fulton.

'Morning, Bill,' he replied. 'Problem?'

'Aye,' Fulton said. 'I'd just arrived at the office this morning when I took a call from DCI Warburton. Apparently, he asked to speak to you. The desk sergeant explained I was early duty officer this weekend.'

'Uh-huh,' Knox said. 'Go on.'

'He asked what time you got in. I told him nine.'

'Something's come up?'

'Yes. Warburton went on to say he'd taken a call from Haddington Police. A man walking his dog on Longniddry beach found the body of a young woman.'

'What time was this?'

'Six o'clock this morning. The area where she was found is known as Longniddry Bents. Warburton asked me to come straight down.'

'You're there now?'

'Yes. Got here just before eight. Uniforms from Haddington had secured the scene.'

Knox said, 'Our forensic team's there?'

'Aye. DI Ed Murray and his assistant DS Liz Beattie.'

'And the pathologist?'

'Mr Turley. Arrived fifteen minutes ago. Mr Murray tented the locus in readiness for the initial examination.'

'I see. Warburton say anything else?'

'Yes. Told me to ring him if the pathologist confirmed it was murder.'

'Has Turley said?'

'I've just had a word with him. He's only had a brief look, but he thinks she's been strangled.'

'You passed that on to Warburton?'

'Aye, just off the phone. He asked me to give you a ring. Said to meet me at the scene.'

Knox checked his watch. '8.25,' he said. 'Where's Longniddry Bents?'

'Drive through Musselburgh, then left at Levenhall. Follow the B1348. It's approximately three miles the other side of Port Seton.'

* * *

Knox arrived at the scene some thirty minutes later. The last two miles consisted of a series of bends which were heavily wooded on the right-hand side. A strip of hilly dunes and grassland obscured the sea view to his left.

After rounding a third bend he came upon a police officer who stood with his back to a gap in the dunes, across which a barrier tape had been stretched. Knox stopped the car, wound down the passenger window, then flashed his warrant card. 'DI Knox,' he said. 'Are the others in there?'

'Yes, sir,' the officer replied. 'If you carry on through the bend you'll come to a lay-by. You can leave your car there.'

Knox parked where the policeman had indicated, opened the car's boot and donned protective coveralls and overshoes, and headed back.

'Find it okay, boss?' Fulton asked when he arrived at the scene. His detective sergeant was heavily built and in his late fifties, and stood near two gorse-covered sand dunes where a forensic tent had been erected.

Knox nodded, then indicated the tent. 'Mr Turley with the body?'

'Aye, boss,' Fulton said. He pointed to the beach beyond, where two officers in coveralls were hunkered over a scattering of rocks. 'They haven't located her handbag yet. Mr Peter Taylor, the guy who found her, didn't see the body at first. It was only when his dog found an item of the woman's make-up – a compact, I think – and dropped it at his feet that he became suspicious. He walked over to the dunes here and discovered her.'

'Hmm,' Knox said. 'I wonder what time the tide goes out.'

'Same thought occurred to me,' Fulton replied. 'So, I asked one of the uniforms after I got here. Ebb tide is at approximately 4.30am.'

'Did Taylor say where his dog found the compact?'

Fulton gestured to the rocks that the forensics officers were examining. 'Where Murray and Beattie are now, I think.'

'So,' Knox said, 'depending on when the victim died, the tide might have been in.'

'I'd say so, boss, yes.'

Knox nodded towards the tent. 'Okay,' he said. 'Maybe it's time to have a word with Mr Turley.'

The detectives walked over to the tent, and Knox pulled back the flysheet.

'Okay to enter, Alex?' Knox said.

'Aye, Jack,' Turley replied. 'Come away. I'm nearly finished.'

Alexander Turley was a stocky, bearded man in late middle age. He was kneeling beside the body of a young girl, which lay supine on a stretch of sand at the centre of the tent. A canvas holdall had been placed at the foot of the corpse, and a large leather instrument bag was positioned at the pathologist's side.

The young woman wore a floral-patterned blouse and a dark-blue skirt that was hitched up to her thighs. A matt of sand-streaked blonde hair framed her lifeless white face.

Knox said, 'How long has she been dead, Alex? Do you know?'

Turley palpated the underside of the woman's left arm. 'Rigor in the smaller muscles just beginning to establish,' he said, then turned to face Knox. 'I reckon five or so hours.'

Knox consulted his watch. 'Sometime after four this morning?'

Turley nodded. 'A reasonable estimate.'

'Any signs of sexual assault?'

Turley shook his head. 'No, Jack. None.' He drew back the woman's skirt and indicated her crotch. 'Her underwear doesn't appear to have been disturbed. I've taken a vaginal swab and it's negative for semen.'

'Bill tells me you thought she'd been strangled?' Knox said.

'I'm almost one hundred per cent sure now,' Turley replied. He pointed to the woman's face. 'There's a series of petechial haemorrhages on her cheeks and in her eyes. When I get around to a full dissection, I'm sure I'll discover fractures of the laryngeal cartilage, the usual marker for strangulation. I'll confirm later, of course, once I carry out a full PM.'

Turley stood and took a sheet from the holdall, covered the woman's body, then opened the tent flap and stepped outside.

The detectives followed, then the officers who'd been examining the beach approached and exchanged greetings with Knox.

DI Ed Murray, like Knox, was of average build and in his mid-forties. DS Liz Beattie was at least ten years younger; a slight, freckle-faced woman with shoulder-length hair.

Murray held up a sealed evidence bag. 'We've been searching for her handbag,' he said. 'But only found some bits and bobs of make-up.'

Beattie nodded agreement. 'Very strong ebb tide this side of the Forth,' she said. 'Most likely carried it out to sea.'

'How far does the tide come in?' Knox asked.

Beattie pointed to the edge of the dunes, twenty feet from where they were standing. 'This side of those rocks,' she said.

'How did her handbag get out there?' Knox said.

'The killer must've thrown it, boss,' Fulton said. 'Making it difficult for us to suss her identity.'

Knox gave a thin smile. 'I realise that, Bill,' he said. 'I was thinking aloud.'

'Might be worth asking Haddington if they can spare some coppers to check the shoreline between here and Aberlady. When the tide comes in again, there's a chance something'll wash back,' Beattie said.

Knox nodded. 'You're right, Liz. I'll get in touch. Meantime I'll get one of the local radio journos to break the story. Someone might have reported her missing, but I'd like to make sure we get a lead on her killer ASAP.'

Murray motioned to the stretch between the beach and the road, where gorse bushes and sand dunes enclosed a central tarmacked area. 'Over there is a designated car park for folk using the beach,' he said, then indicated a score of tyre tracks which criss-crossed a light covering of surface sand. 'As you can see there have been a fair few vehicles here recently, any one of which could have belonged to the killer. Assuming he had transport, that is.'

Knox looked over and studied the tracks, then waved towards the road. 'I think it's safe to assume she was brought here by car,' he said, then glanced back at Murray. 'You'll be checking the tracks anyway?'

Murray nodded. 'Of course. We'll carry out an analysis as a matter of routine.'

The forensics officer had just finished speaking when a horn sounded from the road. They looked over and saw a black hearse-like vehicle straddling the entrance, beside which stood two men in coveralls.

'My assistants,' Turley explained. 'They're here to take the body back to Cowgate Mortuary.'

'You've completed your initial examination, Alex?' Murray asked.

Turley gestured to the forensic tent. 'All I need to see here, anyway.' Then he added, 'Do you need another look, Ed?'

Murray shook his head. 'No, we're finished over there.' He waved to the tracks on the sand-covered tarmac. 'Liz and I will get our equipment and make a start on the tyre prints.'

Knox straightened and nodded to Fulton. 'Okay, Bill and I had better head back to Gayfield Square.' He turned to Turley and said, 'Give you a ring later, Alex? Check for updates?'

Turley nodded. 'Fine, Jack. I should have completed the PM by early afternoon.'

Knox turned back and smiled at Beattie. 'I'll get in touch with Haddington and see if they can scare up some bodies for a search of the beach.' Then to Murray, he added, 'You'll let me know if anything develops, Ed? Either the tide or the tracks?'

'As soon as, Jack,' Murray confirmed. 'I'll give you a bell.'

Chapter Three

'Have we ascertained her identity yet?' Warburton was asking.

He and Knox were sitting at opposite sides of a plain wooden desk in the DCI's office at the farthest corner of the Major Incident Inquiry Room at Gayfield Square Police Station.

'No, sir, not yet. The victim's a girl in her late teens or early twenties. Nothing with the body except her clothes and shoes. DI Murray and DS Beattie recovered some items of make-up near where she was found, but no handbag. We're guessing the killer threw it into the Forth.'

'And presumably the handbag opened and some of its contents spilled out?'

'Looks that way, sir, yes.'

Warburton put on a pair of reading glasses and took a file from his desk, then flipped it open. 'Mmm,' he said. 'Haddington Police interviewed Mr Peter Taylor at length. Says here he left his home at Maynard Road in Longniddry at approximately 5.40am this morning. Joined the beach at the junction of the A198 and B1348 and proceeded west towards Longniddry Bents.

'The tide was out, of course, and his dog had the run of the beach.' Warburton paused and adjusted his glasses. 'The dog stopped opposite sand dunes and began rooting around in the shingle. The animal took something in its mouth, ran back to his owner, and dropped it at his feet.

'Mr Taylor realised it was a make-up compact, and walked over to the rocks where the dog had found it. There he saw several other items – a pocket-mirror, a nail file and a lipstick among them. He became suspicious, then looked to the sand dunes and saw a pair of shoes. He went to investigate and came upon the body.'

'Like I mentioned, sir, it's likely her killer ditched the handbag in an attempt to hamper identification. DS Beattie thinks it might wash ashore somewhere along the coast. I called Haddington on the way back. They've agreed to send some officers to conduct a search.'

'Might prove fruitful, Jack,' Warburton said, 'and there's certainly no harm trying. Meanwhile, though, we'll need every available CID officer on the case without delay. Which is why I've been in touch with the other two members of your team.'

'Hathaway and Mason,' Knox said. 'They're off duty this weekend.'

'*Were* off duty,' Warburton corrected. 'Sorry, Jack, needs must. I've had to bring them in.' He placed his elbows on the table and steepled his fingers. 'But there's more. Due to the seriousness of this case, I thought I'd better consult the boss.'

'The Chief Constable?'

'Yes,' Warburton said. 'And I'm afraid he's of the opinion it should be handled by Police Scotland's head office.'

Knox pulled a face. 'Gartcosh? We're being relegated to second team?'

'Not necessarily, Jack. However, you do realise the predicament? We're at the height of the Festival and the world's media is camped on our doorstep. The force has got to be seen to be pulling out all the stops. Another time, perhaps, he'd have been happy to let us handle it ourselves.'

Knox gave a resigned shrug. 'Who are they sending?'

Warburton returned the folder to the desktop and picked up a spiral-bound notebook. 'Not sure if you know any of them; I certainly don't. They're all based in the west of Scotland.'

He ran a finger down the page and continued, 'There are four: DCI Alan Naismith, the man in charge. The others are DI Charles Reilly, DS Gary Herkiss and DS Arlene McCann.'

Knox shook his head. 'You're right, I don't recognise the names.'

Warburton nodded and checked his watch. 'Okay, it's ten-fifteen. Head Office told me to expect them around noon. I'd appreciate it if you're here when they arrive, Jack. I'd like you to bring Naismith up to speed. The DCI can use my office. I'm being transferred to St Leonard's for the duration.'

Knox took his leave and walked over to Fulton's desk and broke the news. His partner shook his head in dismay. 'So, we're being asked to play second fiddle to our cousins in the west. With four extra bodies I'm surprised the DCI felt the need to call on Mark and Yvonne.'

'According to Warburton, it was the Chief Constable's idea. Hands to the pump and all that.'

Fulton grimaced. 'I imagine they'll be ecstatic.'

'Nature of the job, Bill. You and I have had the same experience.'

Fulton gave a shrug but said nothing.

Knox took out his mobile and flicked through its address book. He found the number he was looking for and pressed *call*.

A few moments later, a voice answered, 'Radio Forth newsroom, Glenn Carnegie speaking.'

'Hi, Glenn, it's Jack Knox.'

13

Carnegie's voice changed; his tone now much friendlier. 'Morning, Jack. How are you?'

'Fine, Glenn. Look, there's been a murder. The body of a young girl was found at Longniddry this morning. Can you run it now if I give you the details? We urgently need to locate her next of kin.'

'Fire away, Jack,' Carnegie said. 'Anything I can do to help.'

* * *

'Call just came in from a Mrs Ellen Fairbairn, boss,' DC Mark Hathaway said.

It was an hour after Radio Forth had broken the story, and Knox and Fulton were at their desks in the Major Incident office. Hathaway was red-haired and in his early thirties, and was seated near the fourth member of the team, DC Yvonne Mason, a trim brunette half a decade younger.

'Switchboard passed it through a minute ago,' Hathaway continued. 'Her daughter, Connie, didn't come home last night.'

'How old is she?' Knox asked.

'Nineteen,' Hathaway said. 'Apparently she phoned her mother just after eleven last night. She and a friend went to a pub in the Grassmarket after work. She told her mother they were going on to a club in the Cowgate and she'd be home after two. That's the last her mother heard. She's tried calling her daughter's mobile but isn't getting an answer.'

Knox nodded. 'Where does Mrs Fairbairn live?'

'Moredun,' Hathaway said. '18 Capercaillie Way. It's near the Royal Infirmary.'

'Okay, Mark,' Knox said, then nodded to Mason. 'Yvonne, will you and Mark drive up there and talk to the woman. See if it's the victim or another misper?'

Mason stood, took a smartphone from her handbag and flicked through some images. She smiled at Knox and nodded. 'Just making sure I had the forensic team's shot of the murdered girl, boss. I'll get Mrs Fairbairn to show me a photo of her daughter.'

'Good,' Knox said. 'Mightn't be her, but it's better to be sure.'

* * *

The Gartcosh team arrived a few minutes after twelve. Naismith led his officers upstairs to the detective suite and popped his head around the door. Knox and Fulton were hunched over their computers, checking messages received in response to Radio Forth's broadcast.

'DI Knox?' he said.

Knox turned, then rose and extended his hand. 'Yes, sir,' he replied. 'I take it you're DCI Naismith?'

Naismith gave a confirmatory nod, shook his hand, then ushered in the others and made introductions. 'Wasn't sure if we were in the right place at first,' he said. 'Thank God for sat nav, eh?'

Knox said, 'You managed to get parked okay? I kept a couple of spaces vacant.'

'Aye, Jack, thanks,' Naismith replied, then waved to the surroundings. 'This is the Major Incident Inquiry office?'

Knox shrugged. 'Afraid so, sir. I daresay it's a bit cramped compared to what you're used to.'

Naismith smiled and shook his head. 'No, Jack, it's fine.' He set down his briefcase and added, 'And it's Alan, by the way.' He gestured to the others, indicating each in turn. 'Charlie, Gary and Arlene. I think it better if we keep it informal, don't you?'

Knox nodded, then gave the Gartcosh team a quick appraisal. The DCI was in his late fifties, lantern-jawed, a good head taller than his colleagues. Despite the warm weather, Knox noticed he was wearing a pair of stout brown leather brogues.

Reilly was around the same age as Knox, but pale-skinned. He sported a pencil moustache so thin Knox's first thought was that it had been drawn on his lip.

Herkiss was a few years younger, heavy-set and, judging by his waistline, looked like he had a weight problem.

Of the four, McCann was the least like a detective, appearing diffident, even reserved.

Knox motioned to Warburton's room. 'Your office is over there, Alan.'

Naismith nodded. 'Thanks,' he said, then rubbed his hands together. 'Okay, to business,' he added, then turned to face Knox. 'I've taken a look at your file, Jack, and I'm quite impressed. You've been in CID since 1993?'

'1992,' Knox said. 'I was a DS in Peebles until 2002, when I applied for a posting to St Leonard's.'

'And you made DI in 2003?'

'Yes.'

'Uh-huh,' Naismith said. 'Your homicide experience is extensive.' He paused and added, 'Okay, Jack, you'll lead the investigation. I'll chip in here at the station, of course – once suspects come in for interview, that sort of thing. My team will work with you, give you every support.'

He glanced at the other Gartcosh officers and said, 'You're all okay with that?'

Herkiss and McCann nodded agreement, but Reilly cleared his throat and said, 'You're sure DI Knox has the right qualifications, sir? I'm not questioning your judgement, but I've successfully concluded four homicides in almost as many months.'

Naismith considered this for a long moment, then replied, 'You're right, Charlie. Both you and Jack are equal in experience and ability.'

He put a hand on Reilly's shoulder. 'No disrespect, son, but Edinburgh is Jack's fiefdom. Local knowledge is an asset that can't be discounted.'

Naismith paused again and added, 'In my opinion, that gives him the edge, don't you agree?'

Reilly's expression made it obvious he wasn't happy with the DCI's decision. Several moments passed, then Naismith repeated, 'Do you *agree*, Charlie?'

Reilly gave a reluctant nod. 'Yes, sir. I agree.'

'Good,' Naismith said, then turned to Knox. 'Now, Jack, the other two members of your team. Hathaway and…?'

'Mason.'

'Aye, Mason. They're chasing up a lead?'

'Gone to talk to a Mrs Fairbairn on the south side of the city. Local radio ran a report on the murdered girl a couple of hours ago. The woman phoned in to say her daughter was missing.'

Chapter Four

18 Capercaillie Way was a small, semi-detached house situated at the end of a cul-de-sac off Moredun Park Road, a stone's throw from the Royal Infirmary.

Hathaway and Mason exited the car and were halfway along the path when the door opened and a middle-aged woman looked out.

'You're police?' she said. 'You've heard from Connie?'

Mason took out her warrant card and held it aloft. 'Mrs Fairbairn?'

'Yes.'

'I'm Detective Constable Mason and this is my colleague, Detective Constable Hathaway.' She gestured towards the entrance. 'Is it okay to come in?'

Mrs Fairbairn held open the door and stood to one side. 'Of course.'

She ushered the detectives into the living room. 'Please,' she said, 'take a seat.'

Mason and Hathaway did so, then Mrs Fairbairn sat on a matching armchair and said, 'I was asking if you'd heard anything.'

Mason shook her head. 'No, not yet.' She motioned to Hathaway. 'Details of your call were passed to my colleague only a short while ago. You said you spoke to your daughter at eleven last night. She mentioned she was going to a club?'

'Yes. She said that she and Shona...' Mrs Fairbairn paused and added, 'Shona – that's her friend's name – were going to a club in the Cowgate.' She shook her head. 'She told me she'd be home after two.'

'Where was Connie when she phoned, did she say?'

Mrs Fairbairn nodded. 'The Quaich pub in the Grassmarket. She and her friend often go there on a Friday after work.'

'Did she say if they'd met anyone?'

'Yes, she told me a couple of lads had asked them. To go to the dancing, I mean.'

Mrs Fairbairn took a tissue from a box on a table next to her chair and clasped it in her lap. 'This girl who was murdered,' she said, her eyes brimming, 'do you think...' She trailed off, tears starting to run down her cheeks.

'Could Connie have spent the night with her friend?' Mason asked gently. 'If they had difficulty getting a taxi?'

Mrs Fairbairn shook her head. 'I don't see why she'd do that,' she replied, dabbing her eyes. 'Shona lives in Portobello, almost as far from the centre of town as we are.'

'You tried phoning her friend?' Hathaway said.

'I don't have her number.'

'Do you know her surname?' Mason asked.

'No, sorry, I don't.' Her lips began to quiver. 'It's not like Connie not to let me know where she is,' she added, then began sobbing. 'Something terrible has happened. I just know it has.'

Mason rose and put a hand on her shoulder. 'Look, Mrs Fairbairn,' she said softly, 'in the wee hours of Saturday morning, the taxi trade is very busy. More so at Festival time. Isn't it just possible they got a cab and went to Shona's place? Perhaps Connie's battery ran down and she couldn't phone and let you know.'

Mrs Fairbairn brightened a little. 'It's possible, I suppose,' she conceded. 'They might have had a wee bit to drink, too. Went straight to bed.'

Mason nodded agreement. 'We'll find out Shona's number, give her a ring. Put your mind at rest.'

'Thank you, dear,' Mrs Fairbairn said, 'That's a comforting thought.'

Mason smiled in response, then suddenly remembered. 'Oh, I'm sorry, I meant to ask. Do you have a photograph of Connie you could let me see?'

Mrs Fairbairn indicated a cabinet at the corner of the room. 'Of course,' she said. 'I'll get it for you.'

* * *

He had a delivery at Pathhead Ford, ten miles south of Edinburgh. The parcel, addressed to a catering company, was marked urgent and had to be delivered by twelve. The storeman signed his docket, and at just after noon he was on the road back to the city.

As he drove along the A68, he began to ruminate on the previous evening.

They had remained in the Quaich until eleven, when Joe suggested they all go to Bungo's, a club in the Cowgate. The women had agreed and they walked the short distance from the pub, arriving soon afterward.

He knew he'd clicked with Connie as she never left his side, either on the dance floor or off. They remained at Bungo's until one, when he offered her a lift home.

Just before they left the club, Shona told them Joe had invited her for a curry at an all-night Indian place in nearby Forrest Road. Shona told Connie not to worry, she'd get a taxi home afterwards.

His van was parked in Merchant Street, a ten-minute walk. When they arrived, he asked if she was interested in taking a drive. She readily agreed and they headed out of town.

Although Connie hadn't had much to drink, she appeared a little tipsy. He suggested stopping off at the beach at Longniddry, where the sea air might revive her. There were parking areas at the sand dunes, he said.

She gave a wry smile – hinting that she knew what was on his mind. Her manner suggested she was quite willing, too.

He parked the van and they lay on the dunes and began necking. He felt a stirring in his loins and began to explore her. She gave a low moan, then felt for his crotch and took him in her hand. As she did so, he quickly detumesced. Then she whispered softly, 'It's okay, John. Don't worry. We'll give it a wee while.'

Then, just like the night at Doonan's, it happened again.

He seemed like an observer: watching as his hands encircled her neck and began squeezing her throat. She attempted to scream, but all that came out was a whimper.

He experienced an overwhelming feeling of euphoria and lost consciousness.

When he came to and saw Connie's lifeless body, he felt remorse. Then the more calculating side of his nature reasserted itself.

He realised he had to flee the scene, and quickly. His victim's handbag lay near her body. He heard the sea pound the shore less than twenty yards distant. He took the bag, heaved it into the ocean, then ran back to the van and drove off.

His thoughts returned to the present and he began to ponder each possibility; various scenarios spooling like a tape in his mind.

It wouldn't take the police long to trace her identity, he reasoned. It wouldn't be long, either, until they discovered he'd been at the Quaich with Connie and the others.

Joe and Shona could identify him, but neither had seen the van, nor knew of its existence. He'd been with Connie when she said goodbye to her friend. She hadn't known then he was driving a van, so it was likely Shona would assume he had a car.

What else might implicate him?

Think.

CCTV! Where – Bungo's? Perhaps. The place had been busy and dark, though; and some kind of artificial smoke had swirled across the dance floor, pervading the premises.

The roads? He couldn't be sure. He had driven via the Old Dalkeith Road, joining the bypass at Sherrifhall Roundabout and the A1 at Old Craighall. He'd stuck with it all the way to the B6363 cut-off, and travelled the same route coming back, avoiding built-up areas. Consciously or unconsciously, he'd taken every precaution… hadn't he?

He nodded to himself as he merged with traffic joining the A772. There was a fair chance he hadn't been picked up by CCTV cameras.

And that was all that he needed.

A fair chance.

* * *

Knox showed Naismith to his office, then took a large whiteboard from a cupboard and placed it near a window. He was in the process of assigning desks to the other Gartcosh detectives when he received Mason's call.

'Mark and I have just had it confirmed, boss,' she told him. 'The victim's name is Connie Fairbairn.'

'You identified her from the photograph?'

'Yes. I checked it with the forensic team's headshot of the deceased. One and the same. No question.'

Knox nodded. 'You're still at Moredun?'

'Uh-huh. Mark and I are in his car, outside Mrs Fairbairn's house. Connie was an only child, and Mrs Fairbairn's husband died a couple of years back. None of her relatives live locally. So, I called St Leonard's and asked them to send down an officer trained in bereavement counselling. She and her colleague just arrived. They're with Mrs Fairbairn now.'

'I see,' Knox said. 'Did Mrs Fairbairn confirm her daughter was at the Quaich last night?'

'Yes.'

'Who with, did she say?'

'A girl called Shona. Mrs Fairbairn doesn't know her surname. They work together at the offices of Standard & Municipal Insurance at the West Port.'

'This Shona, where does she live?'

'Portobello. Mrs Fairbairn doesn't know the address.'

'Did they meet anyone at the Quaich?'

'Yes, Connie told her mother a couple of lads had asked them to Bungo's.'

'Bungo's?'

'A club in the Cowgate.'

'Ah,' Knox said. 'Okay, Yvonne. You and Mark stay put. I'll get onto the pathologist and see if he's completed the PM. If he has, I'll get back to you and arrange for Mrs Fairbairn to identify her daughter.'

'Okay, boss. We'll hang on.'

Knox ended the call, then went to the whiteboard and picked up a marker. He scrawled *Connie Fairbairn* on the top left of the board, then said, 'Okay, folks, it looks like we've got the name of our victim.' He turned to the board again and wrote *Shona* alongside, then tapped the name with the pen and turned to the others. 'And this is her friend who lives in Portobello. As yet we don't know her surname.'

He paused for a moment and continued, 'Ms Fairbairn and Shona work at the offices of a company called Standard & Municipal Insurance in the West Port. Both girls went to the Quaich pub in the Grassmarket last night after work. There they met two men who escorted them to a club called Bungo's in the Cowgate.'

He nodded to Reilly. 'Charlie, I want you to give the company a ring. I'm aware it's a Saturday and you might get their security people. However, you should emphasise the urgency. You want someone in personnel to give us

Shona's surname and address without delay. When they do, I'd like you and Gary to go down and speak to her. I want to know who these men are.'

Knox turned to McCann. 'Arlene, I'd like you to phone Bungo's and see if they have CCTV.'

He motioned to Fulton and added, 'Once they confirm, Bill, I'd like you and Arlene to go over there and take a look at last night's recordings. Check out the Quaich, too, when you're in the area.'

Knox took out his mobile then and flicked through the address book. 'Meantime I'll give our pathologist a ring,' he said. 'I've a feeling I'll be heading to the Cowgate to witness Mrs Fairbairn ID her daughter.'

* * *

Hathaway took a packet of Haribos from the glovebox and proffered it to Mason, who shook her head. 'No thanks,' she said, then nodded towards Mrs Fairbairn's front door. 'She's been with her a while now.'

'Sergeant Cox, the officer from St Leonard's?'

'Mm-hmm.'

Hathaway popped one of the sweets in his mouth, began chewing, then shook his head. 'Don't envy her job. Can't be easy dealing with folk who've just been given the worst kind of news.'

Mason nodded but said nothing.

'So,' Hathaway said, 'the guy must've driven her out of town?'

'Looks that way.'

'She'd have gone willingly?'

'If she fancied him, yes.'

'No possibility of her being murdered elsewhere. Taken to Longniddry and dumped?'

Mason shrugged. 'Not according to the pathologist.'

Her phone rang at that moment and she glanced at the screen and pressed *accept*. 'Boss?'

'Yvonne,' Knox said. 'You're still at Mrs Fairbairn's house?'

'Yes,' Mason replied. 'I told Sergeant Cox's colleague I was awaiting your call.'

'Right,' Knox replied. 'I've just spoken to Mr Turley. He's finished the autopsy. Will you ask Sergeant Cox to bring Mrs Fairbairn up to the Cowgate?' There was a short pause, then he added, 'Say two-thirty? Another half-hour?'

'Okay, boss,' Mason replied. 'You want Mark and me to head back to the office?'

'Yes, Yvonne, please. DCI Reilly and DS Herkiss, two of the Gartcosh crew, have just obtained Shona's address. They're on the way to Portobello to interview her now. Bill and DS Arlene McCann – another member of the head office team – have gone to the club. They'll check CCTV images, see if they can identify the men.

'Oh, and Alan Naismith, the DCI in charge, is still at Gayfield Square. I'd like you and Mark to introduce yourselves when you get back. Get onto the computer afterward and check the HOLMES 2 database. I want to see if there were any incidents reported that might have a bearing on the case.

'By the way, if Mrs Fairbairn confirms the deceased is her daughter, I'll be in touch with the media. I want you and Mark in the office if anything of interest comes in.'

Chapter Five

Knox drove through the traffic lights from Holyrood Road into the Cowgate, then slowed. The City Mortuary was situated a hundred yards along on the left; a two-storey block set back from the road.

He parked his car, walked up a short path to the entrance, and pressed the intercom. He was buzzed inside and greeted by Turley, who took him into an anteroom near the main post-mortem theatre.

The pathologist gestured to a chair. 'Take the weight off for a minute, Jack, my assistant's just gone to bring the body to the viewing room.'

'Mrs Fairbairn's arrived?'

Turley motioned to the partition wall. 'She's with Sergeant Cox and another police officer in the room next door.'

Knox nodded. 'You were telling me on the phone you confirmed strangulation as the cause of death?'

Turley took a folder from a nearby desk, then opened it and glanced at the page. 'Asphyxiation due to strangulation. Fractures of the laryngeal cartilage due to extreme pressure on her throat.' He ran his finger down the page and added, 'Further tests revealed no signs of sexual intercourse, but DI Murray took touch-DNA swabs at the scene. Her clothing has also been passed to Gartcosh forensics for DNA analysis.' He paused, then said, 'Oh, and a check of the underside of her fingernails proved negative for skin fragments.'

'She doesn't appear to have put up much of a struggle?'

'Not to the extent of scratching her attacker, no.'

A telephone on the desk rang and Turley put down the folder and answered. 'She's in the viewing room?' he said. 'Okay. I'll bring them along. Thanks.'

He replaced the receiver and glanced at Knox. 'My assistant,' he said, then pointed to the door. 'We'd better go and fetch her mother.'

Knox followed Turley into the corridor, then the pathologist went to the door of the adjoining room and knocked gently.

A uniformed policewoman answered and Turley said, 'She's ready.'

The officer nodded and opened the door a little further. Knox saw a woman sitting beside an officer with three chevrons on her epaulettes, whom he took to be Cox. Mrs Fairbairn's eyes were stained with tears and her cheeks streaked with mascara.

The sergeant placed a hand on her shoulder and said softly, 'Okay, Grace? We can go now.'

Turley led the group along a short corridor and stopped beside a wide glass window set into the wall, which was curtained on the inside. The adjacent door had a sign marked *Viewing Room*, and halfway up the doorframe was a push-button labelled *Attendant*.

Sergeant Cox positioned Mrs Fairbairn next to the window, then nodded to her colleague, who thumbed the button. A moment later the curtains were pulled back and Knox saw the murder victim upon a trolley on the other side of the glass. A green sheet was drawn down at the top, revealing her head and shoulders. A dressing had been placed around her neck, covering the signs of strangulation.

The victim's mother gave a wail of anguish, then Sergeant Cox placed an arm around her shoulder.

'Oh, Connie… Connie,' Mrs Fairbairn cried. 'My poor, poor wee lassie. Why… in God's name, why?' Her shoulders began to heave, then she convulsed into a fit of sobbing.

Cox inclined her head at her colleague, who pressed the button a second time, then the curtains drew to a close.

Knox went to the grief-stricken woman and said, 'I'm sorry to intrude, Mrs Fairbairn, but my name's Detective Inspector Knox.'

Mrs Fairbairn continued weeping, supported by the sergeant. A few moments passed, then between sobs she said, 'Who?'

'Detective Inspector Knox,' he repeated. 'The officer in charge of the investigation.'

Mrs Fairbairn dabbed her eyes with a tissue and nodded. 'I see.'

'I know it seems like a stupid question to ask in the circumstances, Mrs Fairbairn, but I have to – for our records.' He gestured to the viewing room window, and went on, 'Can you confirm the girl in there is your daughter?'

Mrs Fairbairn gave Knox a look of despair. 'Yes, that's my daughter,' she replied, stifling another sob. 'As I never thought to have seen her.'

* * *

Reilly had little knowledge of Edinburgh and registered Shona's address with the sat nav as soon as he got into his crimson-red BMW 335d. As Herkiss took his place in the passenger seat, he saw his colleague enter the details into the device. 'Used to be my grannie and granddad's favourite,' he said.

'What was?' Reilly said.

'Portobello. Spent a week there almost every Glasgow Fair fortnight during the seventies and early eighties. I'm in a photo with them taken on the beach in 1982.' He shook his head. 'Don't remember it, really. I was three at the time.'

The disembodied voice of the sat nav cut in then, directing Reilly to turn left into London Road. After he complied, he gave Herkiss a sidelong glance. 'What do you think of Naismith's decision?'

'Not sure what you mean, Charlie,' Herkiss said.

'Making Knox lead officer.' Reilly harrumphed and continued, 'What's the point of assigning Gartcosh detectives to an important case, then turning it over to a local plod?'

Herkiss shrugged. 'Oh, I don't know. DI Knox seems capable enough.'

Reilly was silent for a long moment, then gave Herkiss a pointed look. 'Incidentally, sergeant, I'd prefer if you addressed me either as DI Reilly or boss. I know Naismith talked about informality, but I disagree with his views. I think respect for rank is an important element in detective work. A discipline essential to the success of an investigation.'

Herkiss said nothing in reply, then both men lapsed into silence.

Fifteen minutes later, the sat nav announced that they were nearing their destination. As Reilly drove along Portobello High Street, the voice said, '*In one hundred yards, turn left into Pipe Street and take the third opening on your right. You've arrived at Seaview Court.*'

Reilly drove down Pipe Street and turned right into a short roadway giving access to five three-storey blocks of flats. They sat parallel to Portobello promenade and had an uninterrupted view of the Firth of Forth and the Fife coast beyond. Number six was the third block from the junction.

The detectives exited the car and went to the entrance, next to which was an intercom and a list of occupants.

Reilly ran his finger over the names, found the one he was looking for, then thumbed the buzzer. A few moments later, a woman's voice answered, 'Yes?'

'DI Reilly and DS Herkiss. We'd like to speak to Ms Shona Kirkbride.'

'What's it about?'

Reilly ignored the question. 'Are you Shona?'

'Yes.'

'We're police officers. We'd like to have a word with you.'

'Yes, I heard you – what about?'

Reilly cleared his throat impatiently. 'I'll be in a better position to tell you if you'll let us in.'

There was a short silence, then the woman said, 'Okay, I'm on the first floor.'

The buzzer sounded, then the detectives entered and ascended a flight of steps to the first-floor landing.

Shona Kirkbride stood at a door on the left, and was wearing a pale pink dressing gown and no make-up. They showed her their warrant cards, then she gestured to a short hallway behind her. 'I'll talk to you in the kitchen,' she said, 'it's at the top of the hall. I'm afraid the living room's a bit of a mess.'

Reilly nodded and said, 'Okay.'

They went to the kitchen, where Shona pointed to three chairs arranged around a Formica-topped table. 'Please,' she said,' take a seat.'

Reilly fished out a notebook and placed it on the table. 'In answer to your question, Ms Kirkbride, we're here in connection with a young woman called Connie Fairbairn.'

Kirkbride looked at him in surprise. 'Connie?' she said. 'Really? What about her?'

'Her body was found on a beach at Longniddry this morning. She was murdered.'

Shona's face crumpled. 'Murdered?' she said in a tremulous voice.

'You were with her last night at the Quaich pub in the Grassmarket – where you met two men?' Reilly said.

Shona said nothing. It was obvious she was having difficulty accepting what she'd been told.

'Did you meet two men at the Quaich pub last night?' Reilly repeated.

Shona nodded.

'What time did you get there?'

'We were working late, until seven. Had something to eat at a café in Bread Street first. It would've been sometime after eight,' Shona said.

'You'd arranged to meet the men there?'

'No, we were on our own when we arrived.'

'How long–'

Shona interrupted, shaking her head. 'Look, you're sure the woman is Connie? Isn't it possible you've made a mistake?'

'There's no mistake, Ms Kirkbride,' Reilly said, rather harshly. 'Your friend's been identified.'

Shona's eyes started brimming with tears. She took a tissue from the pocket of her dressing gown and began dabbing her eyes.

Herkiss spotted an electric kettle sitting on the worktop opposite. 'What about a cup of tea, hen?' he said. 'There's water in the kettle?'

Shona continued wiping her tears, then said, 'I boiled it before you arrived.'

Herkiss rose and switched on the kettle, which came to the boil immediately. He glanced back at Shona. 'Teabags?'

Shona motioned to a cabinet above the worktop. 'In there with the mugs,' she said, then leaned towards a cupboard at her shoulder and took out teaspoons and a bowl of sugar. She nodded to a refrigerator near the window and added, 'There's milk in the fridge.'

Herkiss retrieved three mugs and placed them on the table, then fetched the milk. Reilly glared at his colleague and pushed his mug away. 'Not for me, sergeant,' he said.

Herkiss shrugged, dropped teabags in the remaining two, then poured. He stirred in milk and sugar, and gave one to Shona. 'There you go, hen,' he said. 'Make you feel better.'

Shona brightened. 'Thanks,' she said, 'that's very kind of you.'

'I was about to ask, Ms Kirkbride,' Reilly said impatiently, 'how long you'd been in the Quaich when you met the two men?'

Shona sipped some tea. 'About half an hour, I think. Joe arrived first, stood at the bar for fifteen minutes or so. John, the guy Connie fancied, came in ten minutes later.'

'He stood at the bar, too?'

'Uh-huh,' Shona replied. 'Connie smiled at him and he smiled back. A few minutes passed, then Joe started talking to him. They came over soon after that, introduced themselves, asked if they could join us.'

'What did you talk about?'

'Movies, music, work. Things like that.'

Reilly scribbled in his notebook. 'Did you have much to drink?'

'Me?' Shona asked.

'No, I meant the four of you.'

Shona shook her head. 'Neither Connie nor I are big drinkers. I had three vodka and tonics; Connie had the same number of daiquiris.'

'And the men?'

'John didn't drink much at all. Lager shandies, I think. Joe was drinking lager. He might've had three or four pints.'

'And at eleven the four of you went to the club?'

'Yes.'

'Who suggested it?'

'Joe.'

'You were equally keen on the idea?'

'You mean all of us?'

Reilly gave a confirmatory nod.

'Yes.'

'What happened after you arrived?'

'It was very busy. We lost sight of John and Connie for a while.'

'What happened then?'

Shona shrugged. 'Not much, really. Around one o'clock, Joe asked me if I'd like to go for a curry. Connie found us then. She told me she and John were leaving, that he'd offered her a lift.'

'He had a car?'

Shona shook her head. 'I never saw it. But I think he must have.'

'How did you get to the club, by taxi?' Reilly asked.

Shona shook her head. 'No, we walked. It's only a short distance from the Grassmarket.'

Reilly made some notes, then Herkiss said, 'This John fella, Shona – what did he look like?'

'Quite handsome,' Shona replied. 'Dark-haired.'

'Height?' Reilly said.

Shona shook her head. 'I'm not sure, exactly. Average, I think.'

Reilly stood and said, 'I'm five foot nine. Taller... shorter?'

'Not quite as tall. Five-seven, maybe.'

Reilly took his seat again and said, 'How old would you say?'

'Around the same age as Joe. Twenty-six, twenty-seven.'

'Did he talk about himself? Where he worked, where he lived?'

'No. The only thing he mentioned was his surname – Masters. He may have told Connie more later, but not while we were in the Quaich.'

Reilly nodded. 'You've arranged to see Joe again?'

'No.' Shona shrugged. 'He's a nice enough guy, but...'

'He did ask you, though? For another date, I mean?' Herkiss said.

Shona nodded. 'He gave me his number. Told me to phone him if I changed my mind.'

'You still have it?' Reilly asked.

'Yes, in my handbag.'

'Could you let me see it, please? I'd like to make a note of it.'

Shona left the kitchen, returning a few moments later. She opened her handbag and removed a scrap of paper, which she laid on the table.

Reilly studied the note for a second or two, then said, 'His surname, I'm not sure if I'm reading this right – it's Turner?'

Shona nodded.

Reilly copied the details and said, 'One more thing. Did you see Ms Fairbairn leave the club with Masters?'

'No,' Shona replied. 'I ran into her in the ladies' room, which is when she told me she was leaving. I said I was going to an Indian restaurant in Forrest Road with Joe and I'd get a taxi home afterward. She said cheerio to me there, saying she'd ring me today.' She stifled a sob. 'That won't be happening now, will it?'

Reilly closed his notebook and rose, then Herkiss followed his lead.

'Okay, Ms Kirkbride,' Reilly said. 'Thanks for your help.' He made for the door and added, 'We'll be in touch if we need to speak to you again.'

Chapter Six

'So, Arlene,' Fulton was saying, 'you've already worked with DCI Naismith?' He steered his Vauxhall Astra from Waverley Bridge into Market Street and added, 'Before Gartcosh, I mean.'

'Yes,' McCann replied. 'Herkiss and I served under him in the old City of Glasgow force, before amalgamation. The three of us were transferred to Gartcosh in 2014.'

'And Charlie Reilly?'

McCann made a face. 'That prick?' she said. 'No, he'd already been there for over two years.'

Fulton shot her a glance as he slowed for traffic lights at the junction of Jeffrey Street and the Royal Mile. 'I gather you don't like him?' he said with a grin.

'Nobody does,' McCann said, shaking her head. 'He's cleared up four murder cases this year already, as he'll tell anyone who'll listen. A man with a *guid conceit* of himself, as the saying goes. And very adept at brown-nosing anyone above the rank of superintendent. You heard Naismith say we should keep it informal. Forget rank, call each other by our Christian names?'

'Aye, I did.'

'Word to the wise, Bill, don't do it with him; he'll pull you up on it.'

She paused for a moment, then shook her head. 'I'd the misfortune to be his passenger coming through on the M8. He gave his ego a good old massage all the way here. Convinced Naismith would give him the run of the case.'

'He raised an objection when Naismith appointed Jack,' Fulton said. 'The DCI put him in his place.'

'Don't think that's the end of it, Bill. He'll find a way to undermine Knox.'

'He's that vindictive?'

McCann nodded. 'As a few at Gartcosh have found to their cost. I told you, the man's not liked.'

Fulton turned into the Cowgate from St Mary's Street, then said, 'You know, Arlene, I've just changed my initial impression.'

'Of who?'

Fulton grinned. 'You.'

'Really,' McCann said, 'and what was that?'

'Well, to be honest, when you arrived in the office this morning, I thought you were reserved, quiet, maybe even a bit—'

McCann interrupted. 'Tight-lipped?'

'Uh-huh, maybe.'

McCann laughed. 'Listen, if you'd spent the better part of an hour listening to Reilly, you'd be silent, too.' She shook her head and added, 'No, Bill, I'm no shrinking violet. However, experience has taught me that every time I join a new team, it's better to not say much until I know exactly who I'm talking to.'

'Like Reilly?'

McCann nodded. 'Like Reilly.'

Bungo's Discotheque in the Cowgate was situated directly underneath an arch of South Bridge, a thoroughfare which had split Edinburgh's Old town into two levels after its creation in 1788. The street lay in a valley created by a west-east divide, which became more marked in 1832, when George IV Bridge spanned its western end, leading to the demolition of many of Edinburgh's medieval streets.

McCann learned this from Fulton, who regarded himself as a bit of a local historian. 'The Cowgate got its name from the cattle which were taken via the street to the Grassmarket, where they were auctioned,' he told McCann as they exited his car. 'Apparently, they were herded along here up to the mid-1800s.'

McCann and Fulton stood beside the Astra, waiting to cross the narrow thoroughfare. A constant stream of traffic flowed in either direction, forcing them to wait. McCann nodded to the road. 'I think I'd sooner have taken my chances with a herd of cows.'

Fulton grinned. He then spotted a gap in the traffic and escorted her across. They jinked around the front of a parked lorry and reached the safety of the pavement, where two men were carrying cases of soft drinks into the club. Fulton pressed a buzzer next to the door, and a moment later a man in his thirties appeared.

'Yeah?' he said.

Fulton flashed his warrant card and said, 'Police. We rang earlier about your CCTV recording – from last night?'

'Ah, right,' the man said. 'I'm the guy you spoke to. Roy Duttine, assistant manager.' He waved behind him. 'My office is along on the right.' He indicated the two men, who were back at the lorry hoisting boxes onto their shoulders. 'I'm taking a delivery of Coke. Please, go along and take a seat. I'll sign for the delivery and join you in a minute.'

Fulton and McCann walked along the corridor and came to an office with the dimensions of a large box room. A small desk sat flush with the top-right corner, behind which was a compact armchair. Two tubular metal chairs had been placed side by side near the door opposite a filing cabinet.

Fulton indicated the chairs. 'I suppose he means these?'

McCann looked at the chairs, upon which a thin film of dust was visible. 'I think I'd rather stand,' she said.

A couple of minutes passed, and then Duttine reappeared, edged past the officers, and took a seat at the desk. 'Sorry about that,' he said. 'Supposed to have been delivered yesterday, but the weather's created a spike in demand.' He shrugged. 'They don't normally work on Saturday, so I suppose I should be grateful.'

Fulton nodded. 'About the CCTV…?'

'Of course,' Duttine replied. He took a laptop computer from a shelf above the desk and a USB cable from a bracket on the wall, then plugged it in and said, 'We've two CCTV cameras. One mounted on the ceiling facing the entrance from above, and the other just inside the club, trained on the dance floor. Both are in fixed positions, so there's not a great deal of coverage.'

He lifted the laptop lid and clicked on the trackpad. The detectives saw two images appear on the screen, arranged diagonally.

Duttine turned to Fulton. 'What time did you say you were interested in?'

'From a little before eleven last night until just after two this morning.'

Duttine clicked a key and a counter at the top right of the screen displayed the date and time: *10/8 – 10.48pm*.

He pressed another key, and one of the windows enlarged, taking up almost all the screen space. The view was from the camera facing the entrance. 'You said on the phone it was four folk together?' he said. 'Two men and two women?'

Fulton nodded. 'Aye, we think they might've arrived just before eleven.' He indicated the counter. 'Maybe it's better to start a bit before then.'

Duttine ran the video back until the counter read *10.44pm*, then began to spool forward. The images displayed at twice normal speed, showing a steady stream of people coming through the entrance: a number of males on their own; groups of girls together; and, more frequently, men and women arriving as couples. In each case there were a few seconds between arrivals. Duttine continued reeling the images until the counter read *10.58pm*, then McCann said, 'There – two couples together. Will you run it back, please? I'd like to see that blonde girl again.'

Duttine wound back to *10.57pm*, then advanced the recording at normal speed. Two females came into view, followed by two men. The women were in their late teens or early twenties; the men five or six years older.

'Stop,' McCann said. The screen froze on the women, then she turned to Fulton and added, 'You've the forensic officer's picture, Bill?'

Fulton nodded, took his smartphone from his pocket, and clicked the images icon. He thumbed through the files, clicked again, and a post-mortem photo of Connie Fairbairn appeared.

He gave the phone to McCann, who nodded. 'It's her,' she said. She turned to Duttine and asked, 'Can you zoom in a little?'

'Sure,' Duttine said, then moved a cursor over the image and clicked, and a close-up appeared on the screen. McCann handed the phone back to Fulton, who glanced at the laptop, then back at his phone. 'Uh-huh,' he said. 'That's her alright.'

McCann gestured to the laptop. 'Can you scroll forward a wee bit, please? I'd like to see the men.'

Duttine tapped the keys again, then the video advanced frame-by-frame until they came into view. The man on the right was looking ahead with a wide grin on his face. He appeared to be sharing a joke with his companion, whose head was inclined, his face out of view.

'Damn,' McCann said. 'The other one seems to be studying the floor.'

'It's how the video's caught him,' Duttine said. 'Pity. But like I said, the cameras are fixed. You've only a two- or three-second view of punters before they're out of shot again.'

'What about the other camera?' Fulton asked.

Duttine manipulated the keyboard and the second window filled the screen. He synchronised the time with that of the entrance camera, then the view switched to the dance floor. The two women reappeared, followed by their escorts.

'Not much better,' Fulton said. 'A good view of the backs of their necks.'

'I'm afraid this side only covers the dance floor. You can't really see the surrounding area. But you can scroll through – might get a clearer image when they're dancing,' Duttine said.

'Okay,' Fulton said. 'We'd better take a look.'

Duttine gave Fulton a puzzled glance, then gestured to the laptop. '10.45pm until 2am?'

'Mmm,' Fulton said. 'I see, more than three hours.' He stroked his chin. 'Can you make us a copy?'

Duttine nodded, then leaned across, pulled a small cardboard box from the shelf and took out a memory stick, which he plugged into the computer. 'You'll be able to cover the entire period,' he said.

'Me?' Fulton said, then shook his head. 'I'm not that good with computers.' He turned to McCann. 'You, Arlene?'

McCann shrugged. 'Not too clever. I've enough of a struggle with my smartphone.'

'Not to worry,' Fulton said. 'We've a young DC called Hathaway who's an expert. He'll figure it out.'

Duttine completed the transfer and handed the USB stick to Fulton. 'One thing, though,' he said, 'I should advise you that there's almost continuous flashing coloured lights on the dance floor – they're synchronised with the music, see? Oh, and the system's linked to a dry ice machine. It produces a smoke-like fog. It'll mean you're only likely to see those who are nearest the camera.'

The detectives exchanged glances, then McCann gave an almost cynical smile. 'Young Hathaway's in for a treat, isn't he?'

Chapter Seven

Mason was the first to see Knox when he arrived back at Gayfield Square. She could tell from his expression that Mrs Fairbairn's identification had proved positive, and confirmed this the moment he drew near her desk.

'It's Connie, boss?'

'Afraid so,' he said, then shook his head. 'You know, the more of these things I attend, the more difficult they are to deal with. Men and women IDing their spouses, parents IDing their kids…' His voice trailed off.

Mason shot him a sympathetic look. 'It's always that way, boss,' she said. 'You never become inured.'

Knox acknowledged this with a philosophical shrug, then promptly changed the subject. He gestured to Naismith's office. 'You and Mark introduced yourselves to the DCI?'

Mason nodded. 'Almost as soon as we got back.'

Knox glanced at Hathaway, who was deeply engrossed with his desktop computer until he looked over his shoulder and registered Knox's presence. 'Hi, boss,' he said, his eyes swivelling back to the screen.

'Found something, Mark?'

'I think so,' Hathaway said, nodding at the display. 'In the last six months there've been fourteen rapes or attempted rapes in the Lothian area. Twenty-three other violent assaults on women. But the one I'm looking at, I missed first time around.'

Knox said, 'Go on.'

'Concerns a twenty-one-year-old woman called Evie Lorimer, who was given a lift home by a man she met. Apparently, he tried to kill her.'

'Where and what time was this?' Knox asked.

Hathaway peered at the screen. 'Approximately 1.30am on 14 July, at a cul-de-sac at Roull Gardens, Inverleith. Lorimer claims she met the man at Doonan's in Market Street. He offered to drive her to her home at Wardie Park View. On the way there, they stopped at Roull Gardens.' Hathaway paused and scrolled the text. 'Says she assumed the stop was for "a kiss and a cuddle". But instead he dragged her into the back of his van and attempted to strangle her. She screamed, which alerted a Mr Gordon Poole, who was walking his dog. After Poole called out, Lorimer was able to escape. It was then that the attacker drove off.'

'Did either she or Mr Poole get his number?'

'No. Only a description of the vehicle and the man driving it.'

'There's more?' Knox said.

Hathaway studied the screen. 'Yes, boss. It's thought the van was a VW Caddy, white or off-white in colour. The man was in his mid-twenties and clean-shaven. Smartly dressed, around five-seven in height.'

'He dragged her into the back of the van?' Mason asked.

Hathaway pointed to the screen. 'So it says in her statement.'

'Okay, Mark,' Knox said. 'Give her a ring, will you? I'd like to talk to her as soon as we can.'

As Hathaway reached for the phone on his desk, Knox turned to Mason. 'Anything else while I was away?'

'Oh, yes – Haddington called. A DI called Ernie Clark.' She went over to her desk and returned with a scrap of paper. 'I made a note.' She read from the paper: '"A team of twenty-two officers have combed the beach between Port Seton and Aberlady. Results are negative. Do you wish to extend the search?"'

Knox shook his head. 'No, I don't think so, Yvonne. Give him a bell, tell him thanks, but we know who the victim is now. Further searches might just be a waste of manpower.'

As Mason headed back to her desk, Knox's mobile began ringing. The screen told him the call was from DI Murray, the forensics officer.

'Hi, Ed,' Knox answered. 'Any luck?'

'With the tyre tracks, yes,' Murray replied. 'Nothing back from forensics yet.'

'Probably Monday before those come through?'

'I think so,' Murray said. 'Either that or late tomorrow.'

'Sorry. You mentioned something about tyre tracks?'

'Yes. We've managed to identify the make of the tyre and the weight of the vehicle.'

'I see. And?'

'We isolated the tread of the last vehicle to use the parking area. The weather was our best ally as there's been little wind in the last 24 hours. Gave a clear impression on the covering of sand.'

'The type of tyre and the vehicle's weight. I take it that's of significance?' Knox said.

'It is, yes. The tyres are made by a company called Byrona. They're Czech. Not stocked by many dealers in the UK – but here's the important thing: they're only made for light commercial vehicles, particularly vans. Those with an unladen or kerb weight of approximately 1,600 kilograms.'

'Mmm,' Knox said. 'So, our killer drove a van?'

'Yes, not huge. Something like a Transit. The make is distinctive by the pattern of its tread. The fact it's a van is backed up with the width of the wheelbase and the degree of impression in the sand. Unlike cars parked at the dunes, the tread cut through to the tarmac.'

Knox nodded. 'Thanks, Ed, that gives us something to go on.' He paused. 'About the DNA – you'll update me when you hear from the lab?'

'As soon as reports come in, Jack.'

'Okay, Ed. Cheers.'

Soon after Knox ended the call, Fulton and McCann entered the office, followed shortly afterward by Reilly and Herkiss. Naismith exited his office and listened in as the detectives made their reports.

After Reilly spoke, Naismith addressed him: 'The man Shona was with, you spoke to him?'

Reilly shook his head. 'No, Alan. The call went straight to voicemail. I got his address via his service provider: 12a Meadowbank Grove. Ms Kirkbride gave me a detailed description of John Masters, the man Fairbairn was with.'

Naismith nodded and turned to Fulton. 'Any luck with the recordings from the club, Bill?'

Fulton shook his head. 'The video's not that clear on one of the men. But we're almost sure it's Masters.' He nodded to Hathaway. 'Mark's going to take a look at the remainder of the tape, see if we can get a clearer image. Unfortunately, the Quaich doesn't have CCTV, so no joy there.'

Naismith glanced at Knox. 'So, this John Masters – not likely his real name, but we'll go with it for the moment – we've a fair idea what he looks like, but no photographic proof. Anything else?'

Knox nodded. 'A couple of things that might prove relevant,' he said, going to Hathaway's desk and tapping the computer, 'Mark got a lead on the HOLMES 2 database: a young woman called Evie Lorimer, assaulted four weeks ago. Her attacker gave her a lift home from a pub called Doonan's in Market Street. She claims the man tried to strangle her—'

Knox paused when Hathaway raised a hand.

'Mark?' Knox said.

'Sorry to interrupt, boss, but I got through to Evie Lorimer on her mobile. She's on holiday in Spain. Won't be back in town until tomorrow. Her plane gets into Edinburgh Airport at 2.55pm.'

'And?'

'I asked if we could speak to her at Wardie Park View after she landed. She said she'd prefer to come into the office. I've arranged to see her at four o'clock.'

'Okay,' Knox said. 'We'll talk to her then.' He turned back to Naismith. 'I think the description Shona gave of Masters is a close match to Lorimer's attacker.' He paused for a moment, and added, 'However, I received an interesting call from DI Murray, our forensics officer. Makes me pretty much a hundred per cent sure he's our man.'

Naismith nodded. 'Really, Jack?' he said. 'Why?'

'Murray photographed a fresh set of tyre prints where Connie's body was found – from the vehicle most likely to have been the killer's. The treads identify a Czech firm who make tyres exclusively for light vans.'

'Very interesting,' Naismith said, giving a slow nod. 'Connie's killer and Lorimer's attacker – a van was at the scene on both occasions.'

Naismith flexed his shoulders and checked his watch. 'Okay, folks,' he said. 'It's almost six. If you'd like to wrap for the night, I'm happy.' He turned to Knox and added, 'We can speak to this Joe fella and Evie Lorimer tomorrow.'

* * *

Knox asked Hathaway if he was willing to remain in the office to check the club recording to the finish. 'Sure, boss,' the young DC replied. 'The mother-in-law is coming tonight anyway.' He rolled his eyes. 'Visiting her new grandson. They won't worry about me being late.'

'Thanks, Mark,' Knox said. 'You can have a long lie-in to compensate. You don't need to come in until noon tomorrow.'

Naismith left soon afterward, followed by Herkiss and McCann. A second or two later, Reilly went to his desk to fetch his briefcase. He turned just as Mason was saying goodnight to Knox.

What particularly piqued his attention was a long moment of eye contact between the two; an almost imperceptible hint that something deeper existed there.

Reilly followed, reaching the street in time to see her get into a dark-green Mini. He watched as she turned right at the roundabout, heading up Leith Street.

The entrance door opened behind him and he turned and saw Knox.

'Off then, Charlie?' Knox said. 'DCI Naismith told me you're staying at the Crowne Plaza on Royal Terrace?'

'Yes,' Reilly replied coldly. Knox waited to see if he was about to add anything, but the DI remained silent.

Knox activated the remote locking, his VW Passat beeped, and its indicators flashed. 'Righto then,' he said. 'See you tomorrow.'

Fulton left the building in time to see Reilly standing on the pavement watching Knox's car turn into Leith Street. 'Okay, boss?' he said.

The Gartcosh detective turned and gave him a supercilious smile. 'Aye, Bill, fine,' he replied. He nodded to his BMW in the official car park. 'I was just wondering whether to leave the car here. It's only a short walk to Royal Terrace.'

'All four of you billeted at the same hotel?' Fulton asked.

'Yes. Beats driving to Rutherglen.'

Fulton fished in his pocket and found his car keys. 'Aye, I suppose it does.' He motioned to his Astra which was parked across the street. 'Ah, well. Better be off. There's a replay of the Newcastle United v Tottenham Hotspur match on Sky tonight. They tell me it wasn't a bad game. I don't want to miss it.'

'I see,' Reilly said. 'Bill – can I ask you something?'

'Yes?'

'Your boss and DC Mason. There's something between them?'

Fulton stopped and turned to face Reilly. 'I'm not sure what you mean.'

'Jack and Yvonne. They're in a relationship?'

'I don't think that's any of my business,' Fulton said. He stabbed a finger at the DI and added, 'And, with respect, boss, I don't think it's yours either.'

* * *

'That Reilly,' Mason said. 'He makes my skin crawl.' She and Knox were in the sitting room of Knox's flat, having recently finished a tikka masala takeaway. Knox stood at the drinks cabinet and poured himself a Macallan single malt. He put back the whisky, took a bottle of Absolut, and splashed a generous measure into a second tumbler. 'Doesn't go out of his way to win any popularity stakes, does he? Bill told me Arlene doesn't like him either.'

'She actually said that?'

Knox placed Mason's drink on a table next to the settee and sat down beside her. 'Yes. Apparently, he's got himself a bit of a reputation at Gartcosh.'

'Really?'

'Mm-hmm.'

'Bill said Reilly wasn't happy when Naismith appointed you to lead the case.'

Knox nodded. 'It was only after the DCI pointed out the advantages on the ground – local knowledge and the like – that he agreed.'

'But he wasn't happy?'

'No, I suppose not.' Knox raised his eyes in a moment of reflection. 'I tried to engage him in conversation on the way home tonight, but he remained unresponsive.'

Mason added some bitter lemon to her glass and took a sip, then said, 'Strange, isn't it?'

'What is?'

'Office politics – Gartcosh. We're lucky here, I suppose. You, me, Bill, and Mark. Warburton, too. Work well as a team. No infighting or anything like that.'

Knox shrugged. 'That's the trouble when you swim with big fish.' He reached over and mock-punched her chin. 'Fair number of sharks in the pool.'

'Exactly why I turned down Warburton's offer to put me up for sergeant last year.'

'You should've gone for it,' Knox said. 'You'd have sailed the selection interviews.'

'Maybe. To what end, though? I'd very likely have been sent to another station. Hell, I might even have been posted to Gartcosh.' Mason shook her head. 'No, I'm happy as I am, thank you.'

'Things change, Yvonne. You might not always feel that way,' Knox said.

She gave him a searching look. 'What does that mean?'

He shrugged. 'Well, you're young. I don't feel the same way about things now as I did at twenty-nine.'

Mason's face took on a sardonic look. 'Really, Jack? You were happily married at that age, remember? Then along came promotion… and divorce.'

Knox downed a mouthful of whisky, then sighed. 'Guess I asked for that one.'

Mason sat forward and placed her drink on the table, then turned and put her arm around his shoulder. 'Sorry, Jack, I didn't mean to…'

He waved a hand dismissively. 'No, Yvonne, you're right. I'm not qualified to give advice on that topic.'

Mason gave him a hug. 'Don't be silly,' she said. 'Things change and sometimes there's nothing we can do about it. None of us can say hand on heart that we're masters of our own destiny.'

They sat in silence for a long moment, then she said, 'How's Susan? You visited at Christmas?'

Knox gave a wistful smile. 'You know, I think she's never been happier. Got a wee flat of her own now, ten minutes' drive from Jamie's place.'

Soon after their divorce in 2007, his ex-wife, Susan, had followed her son, Jamie, and his wife, Anne, and their baby daughter, Lily, to Australia. Jamie, who had qualified as a dentist before leaving Scotland, found a job in Moreton Bay, a suburb of Brisbane, and in the last year had been made a partner in the practice.

'And Lily?' she said. 'She had a birthday recently?'

Knox nodded. 'She's four. Just started attending pre-school classes. Jamie rang me last week. Told me she's delighted to have so many other kids to play with.'

He leaned over and kissed Mason's cheek. 'By the way, I told Jamie about us. He mentioned it to Susan. Last time he phoned, he told me she sends you her regards.'

Mason stared at Knox, open mouthed. 'You told her about us? Really?'

'Really.'

She put her arms around his neck and kissed him. 'We must be getting pretty serious, eh?'

Knox smiled. 'Pretty much.'

Mason grinned, then nodded to the hallway leading to the bedroom. 'Okay. Why don't we do something about it?'

Chapter Eight

When Knox arrived, Naismith was already in the building. Reilly and Herkiss were at their desks, too, as was Mason, who had departed the flat ten minutes before him.

By nine, McCann and Fulton had also arrived, and a minute later the DCI exited his office and addressed the team: 'I took a call from the Chief Constable first thing this morning,' he told them. 'A press conference has been arranged for 2pm. I'd like to make progress before then to enable me to present as optimistic a picture as possible. With that in mind, I'd like to ask Jack to bring us up to speed. If anyone has any suggestions, please feel free to chip in.' He motioned to Knox and said, 'Jack?'

Knox glanced at his notes. 'Thanks, Alan,' he said. 'I asked Mark Hathaway to work late last night in order to study the entire recording from the club; from just before 11pm on Friday until just after 2am on Saturday.

'He left me his report,' Knox continued, 'but I'm sorry to say there's no clear image of Masters. The dance floor is almost entirely obscured throughout.' He turned to Fulton. 'Bungo's assistant manager said something about that, Bill?'

'Aye, boss. It's a dry ice machine. Works in tandem with flashing lights, throws a smoke-like fog over the floor. Duttine told us the CCTV would only pick up those nearest the camera,' Fulton said.

Knox glanced at his notes and nodded. 'Which is exactly what happened when Mark scanned the tape. Only twice does the video give a sighting of Masters, on both occasions with his back to the lens.'

Naismith shrugged. 'The two interviews today, Jack, you're confident they'll yield something?'

'I hope so,' Knox said. 'We're going to see Turner at Meadowbank this morning and Lorimer's coming in at four. She's our strongest lead so far – gave a good description of her attacker.' He waved in Reilly's direction. 'Which tallies with what Charlie got from Kirkbride.'

'Mmm,' Naismith said. 'I gave that a wee bit of thought, Jack. And I've been in touch with DS Bob Lightfoot at Gartcosh. He's our facial composite specialist – photofit in other words. I asked him to come through this afternoon. After we interview Lorimer, he'll talk to her, work up a likeness we can release to the media.'

Knox acknowledged this with a dip of his head and went to the whiteboard, which had been updated with the names of Masters, Turner, Lorimer and Kirkbride. He took a marker and added *Van,* a dash, then *Byrona tyres.*

'We know from DI Murray's photo images that a van was used to transport Connie to Longniddry Bents.' He went on, then capped the marker and tapped on Lorimer's name. 'And the man who attacked Evie drove a van, too. In Connie's case, the tyres were a Czech brand called Byrona. Which begs two further questions. One: what's the business of our killer if he drives a van regularly, and two: who in east central Scotland stocks Byrona tyres?'

'A wide range of professions use light vans: builders, painter-decorators, joiners, glazers – any number of trades,' Reilly said.

Knox nodded. 'You're right, Charlie. But we might be able to narrow it further.' He paused for a long moment and added, 'In Evie Lorimer's case, the van was unlettered.'

'He's self-employed,' McCann said.

'Exactly,' Knox replied. 'And if he doesn't need to advertise the service he provides, the question is why?'

Herkiss shrugged. 'He could be contracted to the firms he works for. Deliveries, maybe?'

'A lot of delivery companies operate liveried vans: DHL, UPS, FedEx,' Reilly said.

'Aye, but many don't,' Fulton offered. 'A lot of online businesses use one-man operators.'

'Yeah, and a lot of the stuff I buy on eBay is delivered by courier vans which are not signwritten,' Mason said.

Knox nodded. 'Okay, we're agreed it's a possibility. Now, tyres. We need to check first with the main distributor of Byrona in the UK; then concentrate on who stocks them in the Lothian area. Next, parcel delivery companies. Find out who uses independent operators; make a list. I realise it's Sunday and you may not get through to everyone. But the more we work the phones today, the less we'll have to tackle tomorrow.'

He gestured to Fulton. 'Right. Bill and I will head down to Meadowbank and speak to Turner. Later, I'd like Arlene and Yvonne to interview Lorimer. I've a hunch she'll respond better to female officers.'

Reilly gave Knox a disgruntled look, then turned to Naismith. 'Shouldn't I be the one to interview Turner, Alan?' he said. 'It was my lead after all.'

Naismith shook his head. 'No, Charlie, I don't think so. We're working as a team, remember? I appreciate your interview with Kirkbride got us off to a good start.' He nodded to Knox. 'But I think we'll let Jack and Bill handle this one.'

Naismith addressed the others. 'Righto,' he said. 'I suggest you commence ringing around: Arlene and

Yvonne – see if you can track down the UK Byrona distributor. Failing that, have a word with tyre fitters – they'll no doubt give you a lead. Charlie and Gary – do as Jack recommends, discover which courier companies use drivers operating a single vehicle.'

Naismith drew Knox aside then and added, 'Get back to me when you've interviewed Turner, will you, Jack? I'd like to know if we've anything new.'

* * *

Knox and Fulton had just settled into the car for the short drive to Meadowbank when Fulton cleared his throat. 'I've something to say to you, boss,' he said. 'And I'm afraid it's a wee bit personal.'

Knox gave his partner a look of curiosity. 'Okay,' he replied. 'Go ahead.'

'About you and Yvonne.'

'What about us?'

Fulton looked uncomfortable. 'Like I say, it's a bit personal.'

'About Yvonne and me being in a relationship, you mean?'

'Well, I– I mean, Hathaway and me…' Fulton paused, searching for the right words.

'You're telling me that you know about it?'

Fulton nodded. 'Aye.'

'There are no secrets in the nick, right? Come on, Bill. I'm well aware that you, Mark and most likely everyone else in the station knows about us. And Yvonne's aware of that, too. So, why're you asking?'

Fulton shook his head. 'Reilly.'

'Reilly?'

'Aye. I was coming out of the station last night after you and Yvonne had gone. Reilly was on the pavement outside, watching you drive off.'

'He said something to you?'

Fulton nodded. 'Asked if you and Yvonne were an item. I told him to mind his own business.'

Knox shook his head in disbelief. 'What a bloody wee sod.'

'I wouldn't treat it lightly, boss. Like I said yesterday, Arlene told me he's gone out of his way to make trouble for others.'

'I can't see why he's curious about me and Yvonne, though. It's not as if a relationship between cops is something out of the ordinary,' Knox said.

Fulton pulled a face. 'It isn't,' he said, 'but he's a devious bugger. Like this morning. Complaining to Naismith because you wanted to interview Turner.'

Knox shrugged. 'So much for being a team player, eh? Not to worry, Bill. I've crossed swords with those types before. Give them enough rope and they end up hanging themselves.'

Knox was driving through Abbeyhill on the final stretch to Meadowbank. He passed a large stand set back off the road, then turned left into Meadowbank Grove, a row of terraced houses backing onto the Velodrome; part of the Meadowbank Stadium complex.

12a was an upper flat accessed by an outside flight of steps. They climbed the stairs. At the top, Knox rang the bell. A moment later, the door was opened by a plump, middle-aged woman wearing a patterned pinafore.

'Yes?' she said brusquely.

Knox showed her his warrant card. 'May I speak to Joe Turner, please?'

'You're police?'

'Yes.'

'What's it about?'

'Are you Joe's mother?'

The woman nodded. 'I am,' she replied, folding her arms. 'He's done nothing wrong.'

'I never said he had, Mrs Turner. May I speak to him, please?'

Mrs Turner gave a reluctant nod, then opened the door wider. 'I suppose so,' she said. 'Come in.'

Knox and Fulton followed her along an L-shaped hallway, then she waved to a room on the right. 'You can take a seat in there,' she said. 'I'll have to get him. He's having a long lie-in.'

The detectives entered a compact sitting room furnished with a beige three-piece suite, a coffee table, and a display cabinet. A flat screen television on the wall facing the settee was tuned to a cooking programme.

Knox and Fulton heard muffled voices coming from another room, then moments later Mrs Turner reappeared with a man in his mid-twenties wearing a dark-green dressing gown over a pair of striped pyjamas. He was slightly built with a pock-marked face, and looked quite hungover.

Mrs Turner took a remote from the table and muted the television, then gestured to the settee. 'Please,' she said, 'take a seat.' Then, to her son, she added, 'These men want to talk to you, Joe. They're detectives.' She gave Knox and Fulton a thin smile and left the room.

Her son indicated the settee and said, 'Okay. I suppose you'd better do as my mum says and take a seat.'

The three of them sat and Turner added, 'Sorry I'm not dressed. I was at a mate's stag do last night and had quite a bit to drink.' He paused and gave the detectives a searching look. 'What was it you wanted to see me about?'

'A young woman called Connie Fairbairn,' Knox replied. 'I believe you met her and her friend at the Quaich pub on Friday night.'

'That's right – Shona. We went to Bungo's afterward.'

'You said "we". There was another man. You know him?'

'John Masters,' Turner said, then shook his head. 'I don't actually *know* him. We met at the Quaich.' He paused for a long moment, then said, 'Sorry, why are you asking me this?'

'Connie Fairbairn's body was found on the beach at Longniddry early yesterday morning. She'd been murdered,' Knox said.

Turner's already white face paled so much Knox thought he was about to retch. 'Murdered? Who in God's name would do that?'

Knox said nothing in reply. He and Fulton stared fixedly at Turner for several seconds, then the penny dropped.

'Masters,' he said. 'You think Masters did it?'

'You said you met him at the Quaich,' Knox said. 'You'd never seen him before then?'

'Never set eyes on him.'

'Tell us about Friday night,' Fulton said. 'What time did you arrive at the pub?'

Turner shook his head. 'About ten past eight. I'm a storeman at Carson's Printers in the Cowgate. Usually I finish at six, but they're busy at the moment. Asked me to do a couple of hours overtime. I clocked out at eight.'

'Was Masters there when you arrived?' Knox said.

'No. He came in about ten minutes later. He took the stool next to mine.'

'Connie and Shona. They were in the pub then?'

Turner nodded. 'Uh-huh. At a table facing the bar.'

'What happened when Masters came in?'

Turner gave Knox a blank stare. 'I'm not sure what you mean.'

'What interaction was there between him and Connie?'

'Not that much to begin with. I'd already clocked the women, see? Shona in particular. When John – Masters – came in, it was quite obvious Connie was keen on him.'

'But he said nothing to her then?' Knox said. 'You told us he sat on a stool at the bar?'

'Yeah, she smiled at him, he smiled back at her. He turned to his pint and became quiet. It occurred to me he might be a bit on the shy side. Like I said, I had my eye on

Shona. So, I struck up a conversation, asked if he fancied chatting them up.'

'What did he say to that?'

'He was up for it. Turned out he wasn't shy at all.'

'Shona told us you suggested going to Bungo's. Did Masters go along with that?'

'Aye, he was game.'

Knox acknowledged this with a nod, then asked, 'Were you aware Masters had transport?'

Turner shook his head. 'No. I thought it strange when Shona told me he was giving Connie a lift. He never mentioned he'd a car. Came as a bit of a surprise.'

'Shona says the four of you separated on arriving at Bungo's. She didn't see Connie again until she was leaving with Masters.'

'Uh-huh,' Turner said. 'The place was packed. Shona and I were dancing most of the time.'

'Okay,' Knox said. 'Finally, Joe, I'd like you to tell us what impression you formed of Masters.'

Turner raised his eyebrows. 'What he looked like, you mean?'

'Not just what he looked like,' Knox replied. 'What general impression he left you with. Personality, any peculiar traits, that sort of thing.'

Turner frowned. 'I remember Connie asking him what his job was. He told her he was self-employed. When she said, "Doing what?" he quickly changed the subject. I don't think he was happy talking about his work.'

'Hmm,' Knox said. 'Would you say he had an outgoing nature?'

Turner nodded. 'Aye, and a good sense of humour. Had the girls laughing a lot of the time. It wasn't the booze making him that way either: he only drank lager and lemonade shandies.'

'How was he dressed?' Fulton asked.

'Shirt and tie; smart suit.' Turner paused for a moment. 'You know, there *was* one thing – I had the impression he'd been in the army.'

'Really?' Knox said.

'Aye. There was an expression he used when we arrived at Bungo's.'

'What was that?'

'He said the place was "gleaming" – army slang for something better than just okay.' Turner waved to a nearby table on which was a framed photograph of himself dressed in army uniform. 'I joined the Territorials at eighteen. Did a spell in Iraq in 2011.'

'You think Masters was in the army?' Fulton said.

'Uh-huh, I do.'

Knox stood and Fulton followed his lead. 'Okay, thanks,' he said. 'We'll be on our way. It's possible we may have to talk to you again, particularly if we need to verify anything.'

Turner rose, pushing back a lick of hair which had drifted onto his forehead. 'I understand.'

Knox went to the door, then turned. 'By the way, Joe. When we arrived, your mother appeared a wee bit defensive. When we asked to speak to you, she was insistent you'd done nothing wrong. You've had dealings with us before?'

Turner gave Knox a shamefaced look. 'When I was seventeen,' he admitted, 'I stole a motorbike at a car park near the Playhouse cinema. Did six months' community service.'

'You've behaved yourself since?' Knox said.

Turner nodded. 'Why I joined the Terries,' he said. 'Straightened me out.'

Chapter Nine

Knox arrived back at Gayfield Square to discover that Mason and McCann had found Scotland's only Byrona dealer.

'Jackson's Garage,' Mason informed him. 'It's in Glenmore Terrace, off Easter Road. They're the sole agent north of the border. Arlene rang them, they've accounts with one courier company and a few independents.'

'Did you talk to the proprietor?' Knox asked.

McCann turned from her desk and said, 'I did. Mr George Lawton. On Sundays he's only open between ten and two. I made an appointment for one o'clock. Enough time to take a note of his client list and get back in time to interview Lorimer.'

Knox glanced at his watch. 'Okay,' he said. 'The two of you better get going.'

As Mason and McCann left the office, Reilly walked over and motioned to the departing women. 'When they discovered the Byrona dealer, I didn't see the point of compiling a more in-depth courier file. What I've been thinking about is the route Masters took from Edinburgh to Longniddry.'

'And?' Knox said.

'Both roads – the A1 and the B1348 – pass through small towns: Musselburgh, Prestonpans and Port Seton. Likely to be a number of businesses equipped with CCTV. A strong bet one of them picked up his van. Might be possible to isolate his registration.'

'You're right,' Knox conceded. 'But it's equally possible he took the bypass. The only one on that stretch is at Old Craighall. I checked this morning and it was out of commission.' He gestured to Reilly and Herkiss's desks. 'Could be worth covering the coast road just the same. You and Gary get on the phones. Find out who has CCTV. Those that are closed you can contact tomorrow.'

He went to Naismith's office and knocked gently.

'Come in,' the DCI responded.

Knox entered and his boss pointed to a chair. 'Take a seat, Jack. You saw Turner?'

'Yes, Alan,' Knox replied. 'He pretty much corroborated Shona Kirkbride's statement. With one difference: Masters might've been in the army.'

'He told Turner that?'

'Not exactly. Masters used army slang in conversation. Gave Turner the idea he'd been a squaddie.'

'Turner was a soldier?'

'Part-time – Territorials.'

'I see.' Naismith drummed his fingers on the desk and added, 'McCann and Mason found the Byrona tyre dealer?'

'Yes, Jackson's Garage in Glenmore Terrace. They're currently speaking to the owner. He has a number of courier clients. Might prove a good lead.'

Naismith shook his head. 'I hope so.' He motioned to the phone. 'The Chief Constable's been on again this morning, anxious for a result. It's my guess the tourism minister's breathing down his neck.'

'What time's the media conference?'

Naismith sighed. 'Just over an hour,' he said. 'And I'm definitely not looking forward to it.'

* * *

'Any indication who the killer is yet, Chief Inspector?' Jackie Lyon was asking. Central Lowland Television's senior news reporter stood at the edge of the police station courtyard flanked by other journalists. Naismith faced them having read a prepared statement. 'No,' he replied. 'But we're pursuing a definite line of inquiry.'

Lyon pressed the point again. 'Do you know what he looks like?'

'We're interviewing someone today who might be able to help,' Naismith said. 'We hope to release a facial composite later this afternoon.'

Lyon thrust her microphone an inch from Naismith's chin. 'A photofit image, you mean?'

'Yes.'

'Then you *do* have an inkling of the killer's identity?'

Naismith shook his head. 'I didn't say that.'

'But surely if you're releasing a photofit you must have a suspect?'

'As I told you a moment ago, we're pursuing a definite line of inquiry and hope to be able to release the photofit soon.'

'It will be someone's description?'

'Yes.'

'So, your witness is a woman who was attacked by the same man? The killer's struck before?'

Naismith realised he'd been wrong-footed. 'I'm sorry,' he said warily. 'I'm not in a position to confirm that at the moment. As I say, the investigation is ongoing. To add anything further at this stage might be prejudicial to our inquiries.'

The DCI thanked the assembled correspondents and turned back into the station.

Lyon swung back to face the camera with a smug look on her face. She had achieved her objective, which, as on previous occasions, had been to portray the police as incompetent. 'Well, that's the latest on the tragic murder at Longniddry,' she said. 'We'll keep you updated if and when there are further developments. This is Jackie Lyon at Gayfield Square Police Station, handing you back to the studio.'

* * *

'That woman has the right name,' Naismith said. 'I feel as if I've just been thrown to the lions.' The DCI was standing near the whiteboard together with Knox and Fulton a few minutes later. Reilly, Herkiss and Hathaway were at their desks, busy with the telephones.

'Sorry, Alan,' Knox said. 'I should've warned you about her.'

Fulton gave a rueful smile. 'Aye,' he said. 'It's not for nothing that she's known as The Rottweiler.'

'Well, she gave me a right bloody savaging and no mistake.' Naismith nodded to his office. 'I expect the Chief'll be ringing again any moment now. And it won't be to praise my performance.'

'I wouldn't worry,' Knox said in a conciliatory tone, 'I've a hunch we'll get something positive from Lorimer. That and the list of couriers who bought Byrona tyres. A break can't be that far away.'

The women detectives entered the office as Knox finished speaking. 'The only Byrona tyres Jackson's have sold so far have been to couriers,' Mason said with a hint of triumph. 'Six with a company, two on their own. We're lucky. The Czechs began importing into the UK only last month. Jackson's is their only Scottish outlet so far.' She looked to McCann for confirmation. 'Arlene?'

McCann took a notebook from her handbag and flipped it open. 'The company's called Bluebird Parcel Services and they've an office in Edinburgh. All of their drivers are sub-contracted.'

'You rang the firm?' Knox said.

'Uh-huh,' McCann said. 'Mr Donald Russell, the guy who runs it, has an office in Merchiston Court.' She turned to Mason. 'That *is* Edinburgh, right?'

'Yeah, near Tollcross,' Mason said.

'Anyway,' McCann continued, 'he lives above the premises. His office is at street level.'

'He's willing to talk to us today?'

McCann dipped her head, then glanced back at the notebook. 'Said he was out at the moment. Expects to be back at three.'

'What are the names of the other two?'

McCann glanced back at the page. 'A Mr Walter Coates, 66 Duns Gardens, Bonnyrigg, and Lee Spence, 88 Water Street, Dalkeith.'

Naismith grinned and said, 'Good work, ladies. That should get the ball rolling.' He glanced at Knox. 'I think we'd better make the couriers a priority, Jack, don't you?'

Knox nodded, then glanced around the room. His eyes lighted on Reilly, who was still working the phones. 'Charlie thought it a good idea to check the east coast route for CCTV,' he explained. 'I think we'll leave him to his endeavours. I'll ask Mark and Gary to see Spence and Coates – Dalkeith and Bonnyrigg are reasonably near each other. Arlene and Yvonne have their meeting at four.' He gestured to Fulton. 'Bill and I will go up and see Russell.'

* * *

Merchiston Court was located a short distance from Tollcross, a staggered junction of converging roads and streets. The Court itself was narrow and cobbled, the properties on either side former garages which had been converted into flats.

As Knox drew to a stop outside number 11, the door opened and an Alsatian dog leapt out. The animal began barking furiously, prancing around the car and baring its teeth. It spotted Fulton and jumped up to the passenger window, snarling menacingly.

A moment later, a man appeared. He was holding a thick leather leash with a muzzle attached.

'Rory!' he shouted. The dog stopped barking, then gave a low whine and crouched submissively. The man slipped on the restraints and turned to the car. 'I'm terribly sorry,' he said. 'I forgot to close the door of the back room. He must've slipped out.'

Fulton lowered the passenger window a crack and flashed his warrant card. 'Mr Russell?' he said.

'Yes,' he replied, then looked at his watch. 'Three o'clock, wasn't it? One of your detectives phoned me earlier?'

Fulton glanced at his own watch. 'Uh-huh,' he said. 'We're ten minutes early.'

'That's okay,' Russell said, then pulled the leash taut. 'If you just give me a minute, I'll put the dog away.'

Russell went inside and reappeared a few moments later. 'He's secure now.' He indicated a room on the left, and added, 'Please come in, my office is in there.'

The detectives followed him into an oblong room. Along the inside wall were two large filing cabinets and a row of shelves filled with lever-arch binders. A large desktop computer took up most of the space on a narrow table near the window opposite, behind which was a plain wooden chair.

'Sorry, not a lot of space in here,' Russell said. 'But if you'll wait a minute, I'll fetch a couple of seats.'

'Please don't bother,' Knox said. 'We don't mind standing.'

Russell went to his desk. 'Detective Sergeant McCann mentioned something about the tyres my couriers are using,' he said.

Knox studied Russell for a long moment. The man had a bookish look, accentuated by thick horn-rimmed glasses. The academic theme was emphasised by a cable-knit cardigan, which he wore over a blue-striped button-down shirt. He was clean shaven, with an angular face and a strong jawline.

'Yes,' Knox said. 'Mr Lawton at Jackson's Garage told us they fitted Byrona tyres to all six vans used by your drivers.'

Russell dipped his head in agreement. 'Yes, I've a contract with George. He recently began stocking the Czech brand. They're thirty-five per cent cheaper than others and equal, if not better, in quality. Jackson's does our servicing, too. We get a very competitive rate. All my couriers use them.'

Russell paused and looked at Knox. 'But that's not why you're asking, is it?'

'No,' Knox replied. 'A young woman was found murdered on the beach at Longniddry yesterday. The vehicle that took her there had a tread unique to Byrona tyres.'

Russell's eyebrows arched. 'Yes, I saw the report of the killing on television.' He shook his head. 'I find it hard to believe one of our couriers could be implicated in a murder, though.'

He took off his glasses and rubbed his eyes. 'You're sure about this tread thing – there's no possibility of a mistake?'

'I'm afraid not,' Knox said. 'Our forensic people are very thorough.'

Russell replaced his glasses and gave Knox a searching look. 'You'll want to speak to my drivers?'

'Yes. I understand there are six working for you?'

'They don't work *for* me.' Russell paused. 'Sorry, the dog, earlier, I didn't catch your names?'

'Detective Inspector Knox and Detective Sergeant Fulton.'

Russell nodded. 'I was saying, Detective Inspector Knox, that each driver is actually self-employed. They own the vans they use. As I said, I'm able to get them discounts on servicing, tyres, that sort of thing.' He gestured to the files on the shelves. 'More importantly, though, I've contracts with most of the top catalogue companies in the

UK.' He paused. 'I should say companies which used to issue catalogues. Nowadays most of their business is conducted online.'

'All your couriers drive light vans?' Fulton said.

'Yes,' Russell replied. 'Ford Transits mainly, though a couple have other makes.'

'There are no others sub-contracted to you – part-timers or the like?'

'No, only the six. Each average a working week of around fifty hours, driving and delivery time included.'

'Okay,' Knox said. 'Could you let me have a list of their names and addresses?'

'Sure,' Russell said, then glanced at the computer screen and tapped on a file marked "Couriers". A list of names appeared on the screen, together with personal details and a record of their vehicles. He clicked again, and a printer under the table whirred into action and spat out two sheets of A4 paper. Russell handed them to Knox and said, 'Was there anything else?'

'No, I think that's all,' Knox said. 'If we need to speak again, we'll be in touch.'

Chapter Ten

Evie Lorimer arrived at Gayfield Square a little after three-thirty. 'My plane from Alicante arrived early,' she told Mason after the desk sergeant brought her upstairs to the detective suite.

Mason shook her hand. 'That's fine,' she said. 'Thanks for agreeing to see us. I'm Detective Constable Mason and this is Detective Sergeant McCann,' she added, gesturing to her colleague. 'We can speak to you now if you're ready.'

Lorimer nodded. 'Okay. Oh, I came straight from the airport. I don't suppose I could have a cup of coffee?'

'Of course. I'll fetch one while DS McCann shows you to the interview room.'

A few minutes later, Lorimer sat facing Mason and McCann across a Formica-topped table. There were three cups of coffee in Styrofoam cups in front of them, which Mason brought from a vending machine in the corridor.

Mason took a sip and smiled at Lorimer, who appeared a little intimidated by her surroundings. 'So, how was Spain?' she said, making an effort to put her interviewee at ease.

Lorimer brightened. 'Absolutely gorgeous,' she replied. 'It's my second time in the Costa Blanca. I was there with two friends. We all work at a boutique in Ocean Terminal.'

Mason nodded, giving Lorimer a quick appraisal. She looked a little older than her twenty-two years. But she was pretty, with a trim figure and high cheekbones.

'Nice to get away for a wee while, isn't it?' McCann said. She took a folder from her lap and placed it on the table, then pointed to a NEAL digital recording machine at her elbow. 'You don't mind if we tape the interview? Just for our records?'

Lorimer appeared more relaxed. She gave a shrug and said, 'No, not at all.'

Mason thumbed to the file McCann had in front of her. 'This is the statement you gave us on 14 July. We're not sure if all the details are correct, which is why we'd like to go over it again.'

'This is about the woman who was found murdered at Longniddry, isn't it? I saw it in the *Sunday Mail* before I left Spain.'

McCann tapped the file and said, 'There's a strong similarity between your assault and the murder of Ms Fairbairn, yes. Anything you can tell us about the attack may prove helpful.'

Lorimer opened her hands in a gesture of cooperation. 'I'll help you any way I can.'

'Thanks, Evie,' Mason said. 'In the report you made to the interviewing officer, you said the man forced you out of the passenger seat and into the back of the van. Is that what happened?'

'Not really,' Lorimer replied. 'Which is why I wanted to speak to you here in the police station.' She pursed her lips. 'Rather than at home. I live with my parents and...'

'We understand,' McCann said softly.

'I didn't want them to know about... you know.'

'It's okay,' Mason said.

The younger woman shook her head. 'I went to the back of the van voluntarily.' She took a quick sip of coffee, then added, 'We'd been necking to begin with.'

'Tell us what happened from the beginning, Evie,' McCann said. 'You met him at Doonan's pub?'

Lorimer nodded. 'I'd gone for a drink with a friend of mine, Louise Petrie. We arrived in Doonan's just after eight. Then around nine Louise took a phone call from her mother. Her father suffered a heart attack and had been taken to the Royal Infirmary.

'I offered to go with her, but she thanked me and said no, her brother was picking her up. After she and her brother left, I was preparing to go too when this guy came over. He began chatting, telling me he'd overheard Louise talking about her father. He was very sympathetic. Offered to buy me another drink and I said okay. We hit it off; ended up staying almost till closing time.'

Lorimer paused. 'The truth is I quite fancied him. As well as being nice, he was very good looking.'

'And when you left, he offered you a lift?' Mason said.

'Yes.'

'What time would that be?'

'Around twelve-thirty, I think.'

McCann glanced at the file. 'It says here he was driving a white VW Caddy, is that right?'

Lorimer nodded. 'The van was white. I didn't know what make it was.'

'The van was parked in Market Street?' Mason said.

'Yes, a short distance from Doonan's. He drove via Broughton Street, turned left into Inverleith Place, then right into a cul-de-sac and parked. Then...' Lorimer suddenly looked ill-at-ease.

'It's okay, Evie,' McCann said. 'There's no need to be embarrassed.'

'Things got a bit, you know, passionate.'

'Uh-huh,' Mason said. 'Go on.'

'He suggested we get in the back of the van to have sex. I took off my briefs, then when he pulled down his trousers, I saw he hadn't, he couldn't...' She looked disconcerted, and her voice trailed off again.

'He couldn't get an erection?' McCann said.

'Mm-hmm,' she said. 'My first thought was not to cause offence. So, I tried to make a joke of it, saying maybe he'd drank too much beer.' Lorimer shook her head. 'That was a mistake – something really weird happened. He gave me a zombie-like stare and totally lost it. He grabbed my throat and began tightening his grip – I couldn't breathe.

'I realised if I didn't stop him quick, he was going to kill me. I kicked out to throw him off, but his hands were like a vice. I threw a punch then, which caught the side of his mouth. He slackened his grip, and I cried out. I was lucky – a man walking his dog heard my scream and shouted something. That was when I managed to escape.'

Mason nodded. 'When he offered you a lift,' she said, 'did he explain why he was driving a van?'

Lorimer shrugged. 'He told me it had something to do with his business.'

'Did he say what kind of business?'

'Said he did contract work for various companies. He didn't go into detail.'

'Did anything in the van give you a clue?'

'I did see something while the interior light was on. A cardboard box marked "Returns". Inside were a few labelled packages.'

'Parcels?' McCann asked.

'Uh-huh,' Lorimer replied.

'Thanks, Evie, that's helpful. A couple of other things.' McCann tapped the folder. 'In your statement you said you weren't sure if his name was Jack. Have you given it any thought since?'

'I have,' Lorimer replied. 'At first he told me his name was John, but said he preferred Jack.' She shook her head.

'I don't think he mentioned his last name, though, and to be honest I never asked.'

'Could it have been Masters?' Mason said.

Lorimer gave Mason a searching look. 'That's the name of the man who murdered the girl at Longniddry, isn't it?'

'Sorry, Evie,' Mason replied. 'I can't confirm that. Why, does it ring a bell?'

Lorimer gazed at the ceiling. 'I've a feeling it does,' she said. 'He might've mentioned it at some point.' She shook her head. 'But I'm not sure.'

McCann glanced at the file again. 'Okay, the general description you gave of him: five-eight, dark-haired, clean shaven, wearing a suit. That's all correct?'

Lorimer nodded. 'Yes, it is.'

McCann closed the folder. 'Thanks, Evie, you've been very helpful. Just one thing before you go. We'd like you to talk to one of my colleagues, Detective Sergeant Lightfoot, he's a facial composite specialist. He'd like you to help him put together an image of the man who assaulted you.'

'A sort of photofit picture, you mean?'

'Yes.'

'I'm willing to do that.' After a short pause, she continued, 'You *do* think it's the same man, don't you?'

'I can't confirm that, Evie,' McCann said.

She held McCann's gaze. 'But you do,' she said. 'I know you do.'

* * *

'It's the same man?' Knox said. He and Fulton had arrived back from their interview at Merchiston and were discussing Lorimer's interview with Mason and McCann.

Mason nodded. 'Arlene and I think so,' she said. 'Evie was unable to confirm the surname, which tallies with what she said in her original statement. At one point, he did tell her his name was John. Everything else in the description checks out. His height is the only discrepancy between her account and Shona's.'

'The parcel returns box Lorimer saw, though,' Fulton said. 'Interesting. Points to it being a courier van.'

'Yes, it does,' Knox said. He looked at Mason and McCann. 'Thanks, both of you. You've done a good job.'

The women went back to their desks and a few minutes later Hathaway and Herkiss entered the office. They spotted Knox and Fulton standing by the whiteboard and walked over. 'Nothing promising from either interview, Jack,' Herkiss said. 'Lee Spence is a woman. Middle-aged, mother of two. She's actually the breadwinner, her husband's disabled.'

'And Coates?' Knox said.

Hathaway pulled a face. 'Not much better I'm afraid. He's sixty-four and on the point of retiring.'

'Hmm. Which leaves us with Russell's list.'

Knox reached over to a table beside the whiteboard and held up the two A4 sheets. 'I'll go over this and plan interviews for tomorrow.' He glanced at his watch. 'Okay, it's almost six. I think we're pretty much done. You lads can knock off for the night.'

As Hathaway and Herkiss turned to leave, Knox motioned to the women detectives and Reilly, who were still at their desks. 'Bill, before you go, will you tell the others they can call it a day? I'll catch up with you all in the morning.'

Knox's phone rang at that moment. He saw it was DI Murray and tapped *accept*. 'Hi, Ed. Something for me?'

'The touch-DNA results have come in,' Murray said. 'Gartcosh still haven't completed tests on the clothing, though.'

'But you got a result?'

'Uh-huh. DS Beattie and I did some swabs at the murder scene. Although Alex Turley didn't find any signs of sexual activity, we followed up with some specimens as a matter of routine.'

'And?'

'Touch-DNA from her throat yielded a result, as did those from her pubic area and breasts. All match – the same individual.'

'Sorry, Ed. Not sure I follow.'

Knox heard Murray clear his throat, then the forensics officer said, 'The killer touched her vagina and breasts before he strangled her.'

'Mmm,' Knox said. 'So, some sexual foreplay, but no actual intercourse?'

'Looks that way.'

'Why?' Knox thought for a moment, then recalled the details of Lorimer's interview. 'Of course,' he said. 'He's impotent.'

'Your interview with the girl who was assaulted, there's a similar MO?' Murray asked.

'Aye,' Knox replied. 'The woman – Ms Evie Lorimer – told us he took her to the back of his van, but couldn't perform. Your touch-DNA tests prove that the killer explored Connie intimately, but didn't have intercourse.'

'Ah,' Murray said. 'I see.'

'But it's more than that, Ed. I think his impotence is linked to the killing. Could be the sexual appetite is there, but when it comes to the crunch…'

'The frustration makes him angry enough to kill?'

'Yes. Lorimer told us when the man realised he couldn't get an erection, his expression changed. His face took on some kind of manic look.'

'One of the markers for a psychotic personality.' Murray said nothing for a long moment, then added, 'Any luck with the tread prints?'

'Only one supplier in Scotland, Jackson's Garage in Glenmore Terrace. We've narrowed it down to six couriers working for a company in Merchiston. We'll take swabs when we see the drivers tomorrow.'

'Fine, Jack. I'll get back onto forensics at Gartcosh. See if I can hurry them along with the clothing.'

'I appreciate it, Ed. Thanks.'

The women detectives sat together at McCann's desk shortly after their interview with Lorimer. Reilly sat a short distance away, ruminating on the day's events.

He'd alerted Knox to the likelihood of the killer's van being picked up by CCTV, a fact which had eluded the hot-shot DI. Yet, what had happened? He'd been indifferent, delegating him to phone around as if it were of no importance.

But it *was* important. In a murder investigation nothing could be overlooked. He'd learned that on more than one occasion. Sometimes it had been the very factor that led to a case being solved.

Then there was Jackson's list. Herkiss and Hathaway had been despatched on some wild goose chase – while Knox kept the more promising lead for himself.

Why wasn't Naismith aware he'd chosen the wrong man? If he'd given me the job, Reilly thought, there would be no time for petty acts of self-aggrandisement.

And what about Mason, the DC he was screwing? Furtively driving off to keep their assignation. Did anyone else at the station know of the affair? Fulton gave every indication he did, so he supposed Hathaway must, too. Were such clandestine capers good for morale? He knew he wouldn't tolerate it with any officer under him.

He heard a clink of glass at McCann's desk then and glanced over. He saw Mason lean towards the DS and nod to a bag at her feet. The younger detective took a bottle of Absolut by the neck and pulled it out just far enough to show her colleague. After putting it back, she partly extracted a second bottle, which looked like malt whisky. She replaced it, then Reilly heard her say, 'Got them at Oddbins at Elm Row earlier. We're having a wee drink later to celebrate his birthday. He's forty-seven tomorrow.'

Mason said something else which Reilly didn't catch, then both women laughed.

So that was it. She was seeing Knox again tonight. Where was his flat? Somewhere on the Southside.

An idea came into his head. If it succeeded, it might take Knox down a peg or two. If it didn't – well, it was likely to throw a cat among the pigeons anyway.

* * *

He sniggered when Central Lowland Television broadcast the photofit image on their late afternoon news bulletin. Good God, was that supposed to be him? For one thing, they'd got the nose wrong; it had a cleft at the tip and the nostrils were too wide. The image also gave his ears more prominence and made his chin wider.

The only thing right had been his eyes, or at least their colour. And maybe the hair: thick and dark, just edging over his ears. Except he'd had it restyled last week; it was completely different now.

He pondered the situation, examining every possibility. The photofit was something he didn't have to worry about. No one was going to point the finger at him on the strength of that image.

But they knew now that he'd been driving a VW Caddy. It hadn't been mentioned on the news broadcast, but the guy at Inverleith would have told them.

Yet it had been traded in a month ago. And they were unlikely to discover his present vehicle, the one he'd used to take the girl to Longniddry.

Think again. What was really the weakest link?

He mulled it over for a few minutes, then it came to him: Willie McGeevor – what if the cops got to him?

When he'd handed over the logbook and £1,500 in cash, McGeevor guaranteed he wouldn't make a paper record of the transaction. His old mate told him he had a trade buyer in Newcastle waiting to take the VW off his hands, no questions asked. Willie had given him the keys and papers for the new van and assured him no record would be made of that, either. The DVLA document listed

McGeevor as the previous owner, but gave his home address, not his business.

Scott Reynolds, McGeevor's partner, hadn't been present and Willie promised he'd never find out. But if police started questioning him about the Caddy and its links to the Lorimer assault, the purchase of his current van might come to light. There was a chance McGeevor would spill the beans… wouldn't he? Yes, of course he would – paper records or not.

And that was his weakest link.

McGeevor.

Chapter Eleven

Reilly checked his watch: 8.05am. He reckoned Mason would be leaving Knox's flat any time now. He'd checked the sat nav to see which route she'd be most likely to take. He guessed it would be via Holyrood Park Road, which girdled the lee of Salisbury Crags; a crescent-shaped formation of cliffs adjacent to Arthur's Seat, the 251-metre extinct volcano at the heart of the city.

The sat nav showed an exit near Abbeyhill, and from there it was only a short drive to Gayfield Square. She would probably choose this in preference to the two other options – a right turn into St Leonard's and the Old Town, or via East Preston Street over the South and North Bridges. Both were guaranteed to have long tailbacks, as the rush hour was now underway.

As Reilly waited, he cast his mind back to the previous night. He had followed Mason out of the building and watched her get into to her Mini. He'd slipped unnoticed into the car park and pursued her via Leith Street. The Sunday evening traffic was light, so he held back, making sure there was a couple of vehicles between his car and hers.

He tailed her over the North and South Bridges, then at Clerk Street she turned left. She steered right at the next set of traffic lights, then left again into Holyrood Park Road. He slowed to a crawl, then watched her make a final turn into East Parkside.

He pulled into the kerb, waited several minutes, then carried on into the street and spotted the Mini. It was parked in a residential bay outside number 139.

Knox had still been in the middle of a call when he left, which meant she must have a key. He shook his head in a gesture of disapproval, then headed back to his hotel and arranged for an early alarm call.

Reilly checked his watch again: 8.10am. The traffic was beginning to build and a steady stream of cars were heading into the park. His BMW was stationary a short distance from the junction of East Parkside, facing Arthur's Seat.

At 8.11am his guess was confirmed when Mason's Mini nosed up to the give-way lines and turned left.

Reilly reached over and opened the glovebox, then took out a pay-as-you-go mobile he'd confiscated in a drugs raid six months earlier. He hadn't reported its acquisition and since its owner was serving a ten-year sentence, there was little chance of its provenance coming to light.

He keyed in 999 and a moment later an operator answered, 'Emergency, which service please?'

'Police,' he said.

Another moment, then: 'Police, how can I help you?'

'I'd like to report the owner of a dark-green Mini. Almost sideswiped my Toyota in Holyrood Park Road. A young woman. She's zig-zagging all over the place.'

'Did you get her registration number, sir?'

'Yes. SWS 5550.'

'In which direction is she heading?'

'Holyrood Park Road from the Commonwealth Pool. I think she's making for the exit at Holyrood Palace.'

'Okay, sir. I'll alert a patrol. May I have your name, please?'

'Mr Gardiner. Phillip Gardiner.'

Reilly ended the call, rolled down the window and tossed the phone into a nearby litter bin, then did a U-turn and made for Gayfield Square via the Bridges.

* * *

Mason stopped at the give-way, waited for a gap in traffic, then turned left into Holyrood Park. She checked her rear-view mirror and noticed a red BMW parked beyond the junction.

Strange, she thought, the car looked exactly like the 335d belonging to DI Reilly. Surely it couldn't be. What would he be doing up here? She shook her head dismissively, then winced.

God, she had the mother of all headaches. They'd had a few drinks to celebrate Knox's birthday and had stayed up until one.

Jack was shaving when she left. He had pecked her cheek, telling her he'd be at the station in forty minutes. They'd laughed; she'd got some foam on her face, which he wiped off with a tissue.

She slowed for a speed bump, and the bounce of the springs made her wince again. *That's what you get for having that extra glass, my girl.* Not to worry, there were some paracetamols in her desk. She'd swallow a couple as soon as she got in.

She drove by Holyrood Palace and the Scottish Parliament, then negotiated a mini-roundabout, which she'd almost cleared when she spotted the blue lights of a traffic car speeding down the Canongate. She carried on into Abbeyhill, then moved left to let it pass. She was surprised when she checked her mirror and saw that it was now at her back.

Mason glanced at the mirror again and saw the driver point to the kerb. They both came to a stop, then the driver's colleague exited and walked to her car.

She rolled down the passenger window and the officer leaned inside.

'Did you just drive through Holyrood Park from the Commonwealth Pool?' he asked.

'Yes,' Mason replied.

'We received a call from a motorist in a Toyota,' he said sharply. 'Claims you were driving erratically. Almost side-swiped his vehicle.'

Mason shook her head. 'That's nonsense,' she said. 'I was driving normally. I never saw a Toyota, never mind nearly side-swiping one.'

'Is this your car?' the officer said.

'Yes.'

'You've your licence with you? Means of identification?'

Mason opened her handbag, took out her warrant card and handed it over. 'Look, I think there's been a mistake,' she said. 'As you can see, I'm a DC attached to Gayfield Square Police Station. I don't have my driving licence with me, but I can provide it if required.'

'Mmm,' the officer said. 'Sorry, DC Mason, but the fact you're a police officer doesn't exempt you from the law.' He handed her back her card. Then, indicating the police vehicle, added, 'Look, I think I can smell alcohol on your breath. I'll need you to sit in the traffic car for a moment. I'd like you to take a breathalyser test.'

Mason did as she was asked and went to the police car. The officer followed, took a breathalyser kit from the dash, and handed it to her. 'I think you know the drill, DC Mason, but I'll repeat it anyway,' he said. 'Take a deep breath and blow into the tube until I tell you to stop.'

Mason inhaled and blew into the device as hard as she could. 'Keep going, keep going,' the officer exhorted. Then a moment later, 'That's it – stop.'

He took back the breathalyser, examined the reading, then shook his head. '23.5 micrograms per 100 millilitres,' he said. 'The limit is 22 micrograms, so you're slightly over.' He looked at her and added, 'DC Mason, I have to caution you that you're under arrest for driving while under the influence of an intoxicating substance.' He glanced at his colleague. 'DC Mason's attached to Gayfield Square Police Station.'

The other policeman, who wore a sergeant's chevrons, said, 'I'm sorry, DC Mason, but we'll need you to take a further test on a more sophisticated machine. You're only 1.5 micrograms over on our device, so the chances are you're still within the legal limit.

'Gayfield Square's the nearest. However, because you're a serving officer at that station we'll take you to Leith.' He nodded to the officer in the passenger seat. 'PC Lyall's charge only remains effective if you fail to pass the second test. You understand?'

Mason nodded. 'I understand.'

'Okay,' he said. 'My name is Sergeant Byers. I should like to point out, though, that even if you're under the limit on the second test, we'll still have to log details of your arrest, which will be passed to a senior officer. He'll decide whether or not any further action is warranted.'

Byers gestured to the Mini. 'PC Lyall will take your car and follow us to Leith. You have your keys?'

'They're in the ignition,' Mason said.

* * *

Twenty minutes later Mason had undergone a second test and was waiting in an anteroom for the result.

Sergeant Byers entered carrying coffee in a Styrofoam cup, which he handed to her. 'I thought you might appreciate this,' he said, smiling.

She murmured her thanks, then he added, 'I take it you had a wee drink last night?'

Mason swallowed a mouthful of coffee. 'Three or four glasses,' she said. 'One or two more than I should've.' She shook her head. 'My boyfriend and I were celebrating his birthday.'

Byres gave a nod of understanding, then smiled again. '1.5 micrograms is only a fraction over. Chances are you'll be clear on the second test.

'Strange thing about the call, though,' Byers continued. 'I asked control to check on the guy who made it but they were unsuccessful. Seems it came from a pay-as-you-go last used in Cambuslang in 2014. Unable to trace it beyond that.'

'Cambuslang?' Mason said.

'Uh-huh,' Byers said. 'Looks like you've been the victim of a prank call.'

Mason recalled the crimson-red BMW she'd seen parked in Holyrood Park Road and grimaced. 'Mm-hmm,' she said. 'Looks like it.'

At that moment, PC Lyall entered the room holding a strip of print-out paper. Mason was relieved to see he was smiling.

'21.5 micrograms,' he said. 'You're clear, DC Mason.' He stretched out his other arm and handed her the car keys. 'Your Mini is parked at a hooded meter about twenty yards along Queen Charlotte Street. You're free to go.'

'Sorry about the report,' Sergeant Byers said. 'But I don't think head office will take any action given the circumstances.'

Chapter Twelve

When Mason arrived at Gayfield Square, Knox was giving a briefing. He acknowledged her arrival, saying, 'Morning, Yvonne. Get caught in traffic?'

Mason's gaze lasered in on Reilly, who stood at his desk with a self-satisfied smirk.

'Something like that, boss,' she replied.

Knox noted the exchange between the two and continued, 'Okay, there's six couriers to interview. I've given priority to those with the closest match to the main criteria: the suspect's age and description.' He picked up a sheet of paper and continued, 'Take a look at the list on your desks. You'll see it relegates three folk to the bottom of the pile. The first is Shafiq Khan, 47. He's married with four children.

'Next in the least-likely camp is Maureen Somerville, 51, two grown-up children, four grandkids. Finally, Deborah Horsefall, single, aged 23.

'Okay, on to those who might meet the criteria. The first is Derek Norton, aged 47. A courier for seven years. Lives with his wife and son at 6 Cochrane Terrace, Newtongrange. Next we have a Ryan Smeaton, 29, married with an infant daughter. Delivering parcels for two years.

His address is 20 Clover Way, Livingston. Finally, the only single man in the group – Todd Mackenzie, aged 24, stays with his parents at 44 Chandler Street, Leith. He's been with Bluebird Parcels since 2013.'

Knox cleared his throat and continued, 'Okay, the interviews. I phoned Norton, Smeaton and Mackenzie and set these up to suit their schedule. Mackenzie does a late shift, starting his deliveries at noon, works till late. I've arranged to see him at eleven this morning. Norton is home for lunch between noon and 2pm, so he can be interviewed then. Smeaton starts early, 7am, so we'll leave him till last. He'll be home after 3pm. Each are to be swabbed for DNA at the conclusion of the interview.

'Because Khan, Somerville and Horsefall are low priority, we can speak to them on the phone to start with. Find out what they were doing on Friday night, what kind of vans they drive, that sort of thing. These calls can be made when we're not seeing the others.'

Knox held up the list. 'Now, who's to see who?' He ran a finger down the names and continued, 'Arlene and Bill, I'd like you to speak to Mackenzie and phone Khan. Charlie and Gary, see Norton and give Somerville a ring. Mark and Yvonne, see Smeaton in person, talk to Horsefall on the phone.' Knox paused. 'Everyone clear?'

There was a collective murmur of assent, then Knox glanced at Mason and jerked his thumb to the corridor. 'Yvonne, could I speak to you a minute?'

After Mason and Knox had exited the room, Knox stopped alongside the drinks vending machine and said, 'When you arrived, I saw you looking daggers at Reilly. What's the problem?'

Mason told him about the police stop and breathalyser, being taken to Leith Police Station for a follow-up test, and the anonymous call made on the untraceable mobile.

'That bastard must've tailed me to your flat last night,' she added. 'He was sitting across from Arlene and me when I showed her the booze I'd bought at Oddbins.

Probably heard me tell her we were having a drink to celebrate your birthday.'

'You saw him when you left East Parkside this morning?'

'Uh-huh. His BMW was sitting there when I turned into the park.'

Knox shook his head in a gesture of disgust. 'What an arsehole.'

Mason waved to the door of the detective suite. 'You're not going to cause a scene, are you, Jack?' she said. 'We can't prove anything.'

'No,' Knox said, 'I'll have a word with him in private.'

Mason touched his arm. 'Be careful,' she said. 'I think he's trying to provoke you into doing something.'

'Don't worry,' Knox said.

They went back into the office where the others were studying the courier lists. Knox glanced around and saw there was an officer missing. He approached Fulton and said, 'Bill, did you see where Reilly went?'

His partner gestured towards the toilets. 'He's in the bog.'

Knox entered the gents and saw Reilly rinsing his hands. As he came through the door, the Gartcosh DI turned to face him. He gave Knox a thin smile and said, 'Had your wee confab with Mason, then?'

Knox felt a sudden sneeze coming on. He extracted a handkerchief from his pocket and a pound coin dropped to the floor. Bending to retrieve it, he spotted a pair of brown brogues beneath the door of the end stall. He straightened up, blew his nose, then returned the coin and handkerchief to his pocket. 'We talked, yes,' Knox replied, adding, 'That was some stunt you pulled.'

Reilly went to the Initial dispenser and gave the towel a couple of tugs. 'They didn't charge her, then?'

'No,' Knox said. 'The device at Leith registered 21.5 micrograms per 100 millilitres.'

'They'll report her arrest,' Reilly said. 'Bound to have an effect if she applies for promotion.'

Knox nodded. 'Sneaky way to go about it, though. Using an untraceable mobile to make the 999 call. Last used in Cambuslang in 2014?'

Reilly nodded. 'Took it off a drug dealer. Virtually untraceable.'

'Why Yvonne?' Knox said. 'After all, it's me you're pissed at. You believe the DCI should have given you the case.'

Reilly finished drying his hands. 'You'd better believe I'm pissed. For one thing, I'm more qualified than you are. Between March and June this year, I solved four murder cases. As for Mason: how much do you think your back-of-the-bike-shed affair contributes to station morale?

'Naismith?' He harrumphed. 'Nothing but a bloody dinosaur. How can discipline be maintained when senior and lower ranks run around calling each other by their Christian names? Police Scotland came into being in 2013. Seems to me there're a few more steps needed to bring it into the twenty-first century.'

Knox said nothing. He let the silence hang for a few moments, then he and Reilly heard the sound of a cubicle door being unsnibbed. Naismith's tall frame emerged from the end stall, then he gave Reilly a withering look.

Reilly spread his hands in a gesture of supplication. 'I– I'm sorry, Alan,' he sputtered. 'I– I didn't mean…'

Naismith pointed to the door. 'My office,' he said. There was a short pause, then he added, 'Now!'

* * *

'Maybe he should've made sure there was nobody in the traps before he opened his,' Fulton was saying.

Knox and his fellow detectives were assembled in the Major Incident Inquiry Room thirty minutes later and Reilly had just departed the building.

Naismith left his office and joined the others. 'As you may be aware,' he said, 'I've dismissed DI Reilly for insubordination and for attempting to bring the reputation of a fellow officer into disrepute.'

He gestured to the whiteboard. 'Meantime, I want us to get back to our priority: this investigation. Obviously, we're a body short.' He turned to Knox. 'You think you'll manage, Jack?'

'Yes, Alan,' Knox replied. 'We've three interviews scheduled and three to follow up. I'll have to make some changes, but I'm sure we'll cope. Bill and I will take the first of these at eleven. I'll reassign the others.'

'Good,' Naismith said, then nodded to his office. 'You can spare a minute before you go?'

Knox followed Naismith into the room and the DCI waved to a chair. 'Reilly tried his damnedest to make things difficult for you, Jack, and I'm sorry. I gather Traffic charged DC Mason on a marginally high reading?'

'Yes. They dropped it once they took her to Leith.'

'Mm-hmm,' Naismith picked up a pen and tapped it on his desk. 'Look, I'll send a report to Gartcosh which will explain the circumstances and highlight Reilly's malfeasance. I've every confidence that'll reduce the likelihood of anything negative being entered on her record.'

'Thank you,' Knox said.

Naismith shook his head. 'You know, I didn't pick him. The appointment came from higher up, a Detective Chief Superintendent Dodds. I thought I could work with him, keep him in line. Proved not to be.' He shrugged. 'One good thing, though. Dodds and other middle-management officers will give him a wide berth once my report goes in.'

* * *

44 Chandler Street was a narrow thoroughfare which led off The Shore at the Water of Leith, a river which had its confluence with the Forth estuary at Leith Docks.

Double-yellow lines excluded all parking, forcing Knox to leave his car in nearby Bernard Street. When he rang the bell, the door was opened by a short, balding man in his mid-sixties.

'You're the polis?' he said. 'Here to see Todd? He told us to expect you.'

Knox and Fulton showed him their warrant cards.

'Come away through,' the man said, waving them inside. 'He's in the kitchen, finishing his breakfast.'

Knox and Fulton followed him along a narrow lobby to the kitchen, where a woman in her late fifties was carrying a plate to the sink. A young man was seated at a wooden table, drinking tea, and looked up as the detectives entered. He was stockily-built and dark-haired, with a square face and ruddy complexion.

He put his mug on the table, then said, 'This is to do with the lassie who was found at Longniddry on Saturday?'

The woman, who Knox took to be his mother, cut in. 'Terrible business,' she said. 'Makes you wonder what the world's coming to.'

Knox looked at the man and said, 'You're Todd Mackenzie?'

The woman said, 'Aye, he's my son.' She indicated the older man, and added, 'And that's his father, Bernie. Used to be in the transport business, too, before he retired. Long distance lorry driver.'

She pointed to a kettle on a worktop next to the sink. 'Would you gentlemen care for a cup of tea?'

'No thanks, Mrs Mackenzie,' Knox replied. 'We had some before we left the office.'

'I see,' she said, then motioned to her husband. 'Come on, Bernie. These men will want to see Todd on his own. Better leave them to it.'

As his parents left the room, Mackenzie waved to a couple of chairs. 'Sorry,' he said. 'You'd better take a seat.'

The officers complied, then Fulton said, 'Not much parking around here. Your van's garaged?'

Mackenzie shook his head. 'No. Lock-ups in this part of Leith cost a fortune to rent. When I'm not working, I park in Mitchell Street, a ten-minute walk. It's quiet and relatively safe. I never leave anything of value in it, of course.'

'What make of van?' Knox asked.

'A Ford Transit. Bought it two years ago.'

'And how long have you been with Bluebird Parcels?'

'Four years,' Mackenzie replied, then added, 'I don't understand, why are you talking to Russell's couriers?'

'We've evidence to suggest that someone working with him was involved in the murder.'

Mackenzie gave Knox a querulous look. 'What evidence?'

'I'm not at liberty to disclose that.'

McKenzie gave a shrug of indifference.

'What did you do before you joined Bluebird?' Knox said.

'Long distance driving, like my dad.' Mackenzie pulled a face. 'Didn't like it. No social life. Always away from home.'

'You've an HGV licence?' Fulton asked.

'Uh-huh,' Mackenzie said. 'Passed the test in 2013.'

'And before you got your HGV?' Knox said.

Mackenzie studied him for a long moment. 'Okay,' he said. 'You'll find out anyway. At eighteen I joined the army. Only lasted eight months. I was kicked out for banjoing a sergeant.'

'You punched him?' Fulton asked.

Mackenzie nodded. 'The sadistic bastard deserved it. I was picked on from the moment I arrived. Always on jankers for one thing or another.'

'Where were you on Friday night?' Knox asked.

'Out for a drink with my mates.'

'Where, specifically?'

Mackenzie bridled. 'Look, if you think I had anything to do with her murder…'

Knox held his gaze. 'Just answer the question, please.'

Mackenzie frowned. 'A couple of places. Nobles in Constitution Street, The King's Head at The Shore.'

'What time did you go out?'

'My last delivery was at eight-thirty. I got home at nine and my ma gave me something to eat. Around nine-thirty.'

'Where was your van then?' Fulton said.

'I told you, Mitchell Street.'

'What time did you park up?' Knox said.

'Around quarter to nine.'

'Where did you make your last delivery?'

'Currie.'

'Currie's on the Lanark Road, a dozen miles the other side of the city. You made it back to Leith in only fifteen minutes?' Knox said.

'I dunno,' Mackenzie said. 'I might've got home a bit later.'

'So, what time *did* you go out?'

'Probably nearer ten.'

'Your mates, who are they?'

'Two guys I've palled about with since I was a kid. John Harper and Rory Adams.'

'You mentioned a couple of pubs. Which one did you visit first?'

'Nobles. John and Rory were there when I arrived.'

'Then you all carried on to The King's Head?' Fulton said.

'Aye.'

'What time did you arrive there?'

'Lemme think… probably around eleven. We stayed an hour or so, then went for an Indian. Headed home about half-one.'

'Okay,' Knox said. 'We'll need to verify that with Harper and Adams. Can you give me their addresses?'

Mackenzie nodded. 'Sure.'

Knox tore a sheaf from his notebook and handed it over together with a pen. After Mackenzie had finished writing, the detective returned both to his pocket and took out a sealed package. 'This is a DNA swab kit,' he told Mackenzie. 'We're asking all Bluebird couriers to take the test. You've no objection?'

'Why would I object?' Mackenzie said. 'I've nothing to worry about.'

A minute or so later, he had completed the test and Knox resealed the kit. 'Okay, Todd,' he said. 'Thanks for your cooperation. We'll be in touch if we need to talk again.'

* * *

'What do you think, boss?' Fulton said when they were back in the car. 'He ticks a couple of boxes. Ex-army, a fair similarity to the photofit image.'

Knox turned the car and headed up Constitution Street. 'Aye,' he replied. 'And he's a bit on the volatile side. Discharged for assault. I wonder if that was his only misdemeanour?'

'But he'd be in Leith when Fairbairn was murdered,' Fulton said. 'If his mates back up his story.'

Knox shook his head. 'I don't think he's our man,' he said. 'I've a hunch the killer's a Jekyll and Hyde type. Mackenzie doesn't give me that impression.'

They lapsed into silence until they reached Leith Walk, then Fulton said, 'You reassigned Arlene and Yvonne to the Newtongrange interview?'

'Uh-huh,' Knox replied, then glanced at his watch. 'They should be there any time now.'

Chapter Thirteen

Newtongrange, on the southern reaches of Edinburgh, was one of many former colliery towns – Loanhead, Bilston and Newcraighall among them – which had changed substantially from the days when the country was dependent on coal.

One of the few legacies of the era were the rows of red-brick dwellings which had housed generations of miners. 6 Cochrane Terrace was now, like its neighbours, a modernised property with a front and back garden, located in the last of eleven parallel streets just a stone's throw from Scotland's National Mining Museum, a former pit which was open to the public.

McCann found a parking spot a few doors along, then she and Mason exited the car and made their way back. On approach they saw a youth dressed in overalls working on a motorbike on a paved section of garden. He was bent over the engine, securing a bolt with a spanner.

Mason cleared her throat. 'Excuse me,' she said.

The young man turned and glanced at the detectives. 'Aye?' he said.

'We're looking for Mr Derek Norton,' McCann said.

He threw the spanner in a toolbox, then picked up a rag and wiped his hands. 'You're here to see my dad?'

'Yes,' Mason said. 'We're police. We made an appointment?'

A fleeting look of concern came over his face, then he regained his composure. 'Oh,' he said, pointing towards the door. 'He's in. Just ring the bell.' He turned back to the bike and reached into the toolbox.

The detectives exchanged looks, then McCann pressed the bell.

A tall, dark-haired man opened the door and gave the officers a look of surprise. 'Yes?' he said.

'You're Derek Norton?'

'Uh-huh.'

The officers showed him their warrant cards. 'Detective Sergeant McCann and Detective Constable Mason,' McCann said. 'I believe you're expecting us?'

'Oh,' Norton said. 'I didn't think it would be women.' Then, realising the remark might be taken as sexist, quickly added, 'Sorry, I don't mean to cause offence...'

McCann gave him a patronising smile. 'None taken.'

Norton gestured to the hallway. 'Come in,' he said. 'The sitting room's on your left.'

The detectives entered and Norton ushered them into a room with a wide picture window. A large Persian carpet covered a parquet floor, on which two sofas were arranged at right angles opposite a white marble fireplace.

'If you'll take a seat, I'll nip through to the kitchen and ask my wife to get you a coffee,' Norton said.

McCann shook her head. 'Not for me, thanks,' she said.

Mason added, 'Nor me, thanks.'

'Okay,' Norton said. He took a seat opposite them and made an open-handed gesture. 'Inspector Knott said on the phone you wanted to speak to me in connection with the murder in Port Seton?'

Mason nodded. 'Inspector Knox,' she corrected. 'The woman was found at Longniddry.'

'Oh, sorry. Saw it on the telly yesterday. I knew it was somewhere down the coast.' He shook his head. 'Inspector Knox said a Bluebird van might be involved?'

'We believe so, yes,' McCann replied.

Mason took out her notebook and said, 'Could we begin by asking where you were between 9pm on Friday and 2am on Saturday morning?'

Norton nodded. 'That's easy,' he said. 'I was here, at home.'

'You were delivering on Friday?' McCann asked.

'Uh-huh. My last drop was at Sighthill at six-thirty. I drove home via the bypass. Got back around 7pm. Had my dinner, then the wife and I stayed in, watching telly.'

'You didn't go out again later? For a drink, perhaps?' Mason asked.

Norton shook his head emphatically. 'No, I don't drink. Neither does my wife.'

'Your van,' McCann said, 'it was parked here?'

Norton gestured to the window. 'Sitting in the street, where I normally leave it. Not always in the same place, mind.'

'What make of van is it?'

'You didn't see it when you arrived?' Norton asked.

'No. Our attention was drawn to a young man fixing a motorbike,' Mason said.

'Oh, that's my son, Jeff,' Norton said. 'He bought a used Kawasaki Z900 a few months back. Loves to tinker with it. He's quite the mechanic.'

'Mm-hmm,' McCann said. 'I was asking what kind of van you had?'

'Oh, sorry. A Peugeot Boxer. It's parked just over the road.'

'I see,' McCann said. 'And you've told us it was there all Friday night. Is there anyone who can vouch for that? Outside your family, I mean.'

Norton nodded. 'A couple of neighbours opposite. Dougie Newman at number seven and Tommy Simms at nine. They're both keen gardeners. Tommy was trimming his hedges and Dougie was weeding. Both were out until late. They would have seen the van there.'

'Okay, Mr Norton,' Mason said. 'Thanks for agreeing to talk to us during your lunch break. I've just one more question.'

'Ask away.'

'I wondered if you'd ever been in the army.'

'Me?' Norton said, shaking his head. 'No. I was a member of the Boy's Brigade in my youth.' He grinned. 'I don't suppose that counts?'

Mason shook her head. 'No, I'm afraid it doesn't.'

McCann opened her handbag and removed a DNA test kit. 'One final thing,' she said. 'We'd like all Bluebird courier drivers to take a DNA test. You're okay with that?'

Norton glanced at the package. 'How does it work?' he asked.

'Simple procedure,' McCann replied. 'It's just like a cocktail stick with a swab attached. We need you to roll it around inside your cheeks. Takes around a minute.'

'Uh-huh,' Norton said. 'Okay.'

* * *

'Did you catch the look on Jeff Norton's face when we said we were cops?' Mason said. She and her colleague were back in the car a few minutes later. McCann had just joined the A7 and was heading for Edinburgh.

'Yep, A definite look of guilt.'

'His father, Derek,' Mason mused. 'You think his story's kosher?'

McCann shrugged. 'No reason at this point to believe otherwise. We'll find out for sure when the DNA results come back.'

* * *

He knew G&S Motors was quiet on a Monday. Saturdays and Sundays in the motor trade were always the busiest, with sales building as the week progressed. He also knew that McGeevor took a lunch break between 1 and 2pm, and that his partner, Scott Reynolds, never worked on the first day of the week.

He parked a short distance from the premises, which occupied a corner lot next to a stretch of land that was being developed for housing, then checked to make sure he wasn't observed. However, there was little traffic, and even fewer pedestrians. The builders at the adjacent site, too, appeared to be having their lunch break.

He strolled past a number of vans on the forecourt whose windscreens were stickered with prices, then carried on to the portacabin which served as an office. Glancing at the window, he noticed a large card lettered in black: CLOSED FOR LUNCH (1PM TO 2PM).

He knocked, and moments later was met with a gruff reply, 'We're closed for lunch. Come back at two.'

'It's John,' he said.

'John?'

'Come on, Willie,' he said. 'Don't tell me you don't recognise my voice.'

He heard footsteps, then the door was unlocked and McGeevor poked his head out. He was a slightly-built man in his mid-thirties, who wore his thinning hair in a comb-over style.

'Sorry, John. I was in the back. Didn't hear you clearly.' He paused, then added, 'Problem with the van?'

'No, Willie. Everything's fine. I came to ask about the paperwork. Can you spare a couple of minutes?'

'Sure,' McGeevor replied. 'Come in.'

They entered the portacabin, then McGeevor locked the door behind them. 'Monday's normally quiet,' he said, looking at the forecourt. 'Still get the odd tyre-kicker sniffing about, though.'

McGeevor went to the rear of the unit, then pulled a chair from the wall and placed it in front of a small desk. He motioned to the chair and went around the desk and sat down. 'Take a seat,' he said. 'You mentioned something about paperwork?'

'I did, yes. The VW Caddy you took in part exchange for the Transit you sold me. You told me you had a trade buyer in Newcastle?'

'Aye, Manny Calder. One of his guys collected it the same week,' he replied.

'You told me he'd ring it for you. Give it a new identity?'

'Yeah,' McGeevor said. 'New VIN plate, new registration, new logbook. You told me you wanted it that way?'

'I did,' he said. 'And the transaction, you never recorded it on your books?'

McGeevor shook his head. 'No. No paperwork. No receipts.'

'That's good, Willie,' he said. 'And the Transit I bought from you, you didn't make a record of that, either?'

McGeevor nodded. 'Just like I said at the time. The van was, and still is, registered to me. And I never made a record of the sale.'

'The logbook. You've informed the DVLA about the change of ownership?'

McGeevor shook his head. 'No. I haven't got around to that yet.' He paused and studied his interlocutor for a long moment. 'Look, John, I knew there was some reason you wanted to ditch the VW on the QT. I was glad to help out, no questions asked. You're an old mate after all. I don't understand why you're here today, though. Don't you trust me?'

He held McGeevor's gaze, then shook his head. 'Oh, I trust you, Willie. I just wanted to hear what you'd done about the Transit.'

'I told you, John, I have the logbook. It's still registered to me.'

'Which is what I wanted to make sure of. And to confirm you made no record of the Caddy transaction, of course.'

'I say again, John, no records exist. You've my word on that.'

'Good,' he said. 'Which leaves only one thing.'

McGeevor gave him an inquiring look. 'Sorry, John, I don't understand. What thing?'

'You, Willie,' he said, then reached into his pocket, took out a pistol and pointed it at McGeevor.

'What the hell's that?' McGeevor said.

'What does it look like, Willie?'

'A gun?'

'Aye, Willie. That's what it is. A Glock 17 to be exact.'

'You're not serious, surely?'

'Deadly.'

McGeevor began to shake visibly. 'You're not going to…'

He indicated a small room behind McGeevor. 'You keep a safe in there, Willie?'

McGeevor turned and followed his gaze. 'A– aye, I do,' he stuttered. 'But there's hardly anything in it. A few hundred pounds… look, John, if you need some money, I'd be happy to give it to you.' He stared at the revolver, his face now as white as a sheet. 'Jesus, man, put that gun away.'

'Open the safe, Willie, and take out the cash.'

McGeevor stood. 'O– Okay.'

'Remember I'm at your back, Willie.'

McGeevor went into the cupboard-sized room and dialled some numbers at the front of a small metal safe. He pulled open the door, took out a cash box and raised the lid, then extracted a wad of banknotes, which he handed over. 'Like I told you, John, there's only a few hundred…'

Those were McGeevor's last words. His killer pulled the trigger and the cartridge ignited, sending a bullet spiralling into his victim's neck.

Chapter Fourteen

'Just as well we've got sat nav, eh?' Herkiss said as he and Hathaway negotiated a maze of flyovers, roundabouts and underpasses as they drew nearer their destination.

'I suppose if you're local, you get used to it,' Hathaway said. 'My wife's sister lives here and she knows the place like the back of her hand.'

The sat nav took him through a final series of roundabouts, then instructed him to turn left. 20 Clover Way was located on the top left corner of a cul-de-sac but was easy to find, as Smeaton's dark-blue Transit was parked outside.

The door was answered by a red-haired woman in her late twenties, who had a baby in her arms.

'DC Hathaway and DS Herkiss,' Hathaway said. 'We're here to see Ryan?'

The woman opened the door wider, then stood back. 'Yes,' she said. 'He told me to expect you.' She waved towards the hallway. 'The living room's on your right. Just go in and take a seat, He's upstairs, changing out of his overalls. I'll tell him you're here.'

The detectives went into the living room, which was furnished with a check-patterned three-piece suite and a large wall unit. A long bookcase stood with its back to the opposite wall, and a writing desk took up most of the space next to the window, on top of which was a desktop computer.

As Smeaton entered, Herkiss was over by the bookcase, checking the titles on the spines of a row of books, all on the subject of military history.

Smeaton indicated the volumes. 'My hobby,' he said, then motioned to the computer. 'Do a bit of writing in my spare time. I contribute articles to magazines.' He was dark-haired, with high cheekbones and a dimpled chin.

Herkiss nodded. 'Aye?' he said. 'I'm a bit of a World War II buff myself.'

Smeaton gestured to the sofa. 'Sorry, I'm forgetting my manners. Won't you sit down?'

The detectives did so, then Smeaton said, 'Would you like a cup of tea? My wife's making some.'

'Aye, I wouldn't mind, thanks,' Herkiss replied. Then to Hathaway, he said, 'Mark?'

Hathaway nodded. 'Yes, please.'

A couple of minutes later, Smeaton's wife brought in a tray with a pot of tea, three cups and saucers, a sugar bowl and milk jug, together with a plate of biscuits. She set down the tray on a table in front of the settee. 'Please, help yourselves,' she said.

The men filled their cups, added milk and sugar, then Smeaton said, 'The officer who phoned said a Bluebird van might be involved in the murder at Longniddry?'

Herkiss swallowed a mouthful of tea, then replaced his cup on the saucer. 'We think so, yes.'

'You'll be wanting to know where I was at the time?'

Herkiss had just bitten into a biscuit, so Hathaway answered, 'Yes. If you could tell us where you were between 9pm on Friday and 2am on Saturday, that would be helpful.'

Smeaton nodded. 'My van packed in on Friday,' he said. 'Fuel pump. I called Jackson's Garage but they couldn't send anyone out until Saturday morning.'

'Where was the van during that time?' Hathaway said.

'Parked at the Lanark Road where it broke down,' Smeaton said. 'Luckily, I'd delivered my last parcel at Redhall and was on my way home.'

'I see,' Herkiss said. 'How did you get back here?'

'I phoned a taxi,' Smeaton replied. 'I checked Jackson's in the morning and they told me a mechanic was on his way. I phoned another taxi and went to meet him.'

'What time did you arrive home?' Hathaway asked.

'Just after 4pm, I think. I didn't go out again until I met Jackson's mechanic on Saturday.'

'It was just you and your wife at home on Friday night?' Hathaway said.

'Yes,' Smeaton replied. 'And Caoimhe, of course.'

'Kay–?'

'My baby daughter, Caoimhe. C-A-O-I-M-H-E. It's Irish. Pronounced Kay-vuh.'

'Oh, I see,' Hathaway said.

Herkiss cleared his throat. 'The reason my colleague is asking,' he said, 'is to see if anyone can corroborate the fact that you were at home.'

Smeaton thought for a moment. 'No,' he said. 'Only my wife.'

'Uh-huh,' Herkiss said. 'One final question. Did you ever serve in the army?'

'Yes, I was in the Paras for seven years – 2007 until 2014. Why? Does the killer have a military connection?'

'To be honest, we're not sure. He may have, but it's equally possible he may not.'

Smeaton nodded but said nothing.

Herkiss drained his cup and placed it back on the saucer. 'Well, Ryan, I think that only leaves us to request a sample of your DNA.' He took a kit from his pocket. 'We're asking all Russell's couriers, you understand?'

'That's okay,' Smeaton said. 'I'm happy to oblige.'

* * *

Soon after they re-joined the M8, Hathaway shook his head. 'He hasn't an alibi, has he?' he said.

'No, he hasn't,' Herkiss replied. 'The only one who can vouch for Smeaton is his wife.' He shrugged. 'His van might have broken down, but then again it might not. Nothing to prove the fuel pump had gone. If he knows anything about engines, he could've disabled it before Jackson's guy arrived.'

'His phone call to the garage on Friday afternoon? He would have to have known they wouldn't come out until Saturday.'

'But what if he was aware of that? Or didn't make the call?'

Hathaway glanced at his rear-view mirror and indicated to overtake a lorry. 'Aye,' he said. 'We'll need to check with Jackson's.'

* * *

Knox and Fulton returned to the office after their interview with Mackenzie, then telephoned the three low-priority couriers. The first was Shafiq Khan, who he discovered had attended a fortieth wedding anniversary dinner at the Grosvenor Hotel for his mother and father, who'd flown over from Pakistan to share the celebration with their extended family. Khan had finished his deliveries at noon on Friday and was at the hotel with his relatives until early Saturday morning.

Fulton phoned Maureen Somerville, who told him she was keen on amateur dramatics and music. He discovered she'd also been out on Friday evening, taking part in a rehearsal of Gilbert and Sullivan's *The Mikado* at the Little Theatre in the Pleasance, which had lasted until 1am.

Which only left Deborah Horsefall who, it turned out, hadn't been in Edinburgh at all. She'd completed her last batch of deliveries on Thursday, catching an early train on Friday to visit her parents in Macclesfield.

Knox had only finished speaking to Horsefall when Naismith exited his office and walked briskly to his desk. 'Just off the phone with DCS Ross Miller at Gartcosh,' he told Knox. 'One of the partners of Broxburn van dealership was found dead this afternoon. Shot in the head. When the details were entered into HOLMES 2, it flagged up the Fairbairn case.'

'The Gartcosh forensics team is there?' Knox said.

Naismith shook his head. 'No. Only the Gartcosh Ballistics team. Because of the possible connection, I asked Miller to allow DI Murray and DS Beattie to do the forensics. I also asked for the body to be taken to the Cowgate for the post-mortem and for Mr Turley to attend the scene. He's agreed.'

'Did he say who the victim is?'

'Aye, a William McGeevor. West Lothian Police have been in touch with his business partner, Scott Reynolds. They've arranged for him to meet us at the scene.'

* * *

Naismith, Knox and Fulton arrived at Broxburn forty minutes later. Knox texted the others en route, asking them to make sure the DNA specimens were picked up by the lab for immediate analysis.

Fulton came to a halt near G&S Motors' forecourt, then the officers exited, suited up in sterile gear, and walked the short distance to the crime scene. Naismith went over to the young PC on watch and flashed his warrant card. 'Who's the officer in charge, son?' he said.

The PC waved to the office. 'Inspector Peter Quinn, sir. He's inside with the forensics people. Pathologist's there, too. He arrived a few minutes ago.'

The officer raised the barrier tape and Naismith, Knox and Fulton ducked beneath and went to the portacabin.

Naismith's knock was answered by a man who was also wearing protective clothing.

'Inspector Quinn?'

'Yes?'

The detectives showed their IDs, then Naismith made introductions. Knox glanced beyond Quinn and saw a group of people gathered around the door of a small office at the top left corner. Two spotlights illuminated the scene, their cables linked via a window fanlight to a generator outside.

Knox was able to discern pathologist Alex Turley crouched over the body of a man who was lying prone. Also near the victim were DI Murray, DS Beattie and two other officers he assumed were ballistic specialists.

'Who found him and when, Peter?' Naismith was asking.

'A man called Alistair MacLeod. Went to the office to inquire about a van just after two. The door was open, but he knocked anyway. When nobody answered, he entered and found McGeevor lying in a pool of blood.'

'Anyone hear or see anything?'

'So far we've only been able to talk to builders at the adjacent site,' Quinn replied. 'One of them heard a bang he assumed was a car backfiring. He reckons that was around ten past one. Nobody saw anyone.'

'Does there appear to have been a motive?'

'Yes. McGeevor was shot after opening his safe. There's an empty cash box on the floor beside him.'

Naismith nodded. 'McGeevor's partner, Scott Reynolds – he's here yet?'

'No, sir.' Quinn motioned to the officer standing by the barrier tape. 'I've asked PC Cullen to let me know when he arrives.'

Naismith gestured to the forensic officers and the pathologist. 'How long have they been with the body?'

Quinn checked his watch. 'The ballistics people were the first. They've been here around an hour. DI Murray and DS Beattie arrived a half hour ago. Mr Turley was just ahead of you.'

Knox saw some movement in the corner, then the ballistics officers separated from the others and came to the door.

'This is DI June Short and DI Brian Fraser,' Quinn told Naismith. 'Ballistic Forensics.'

Naismith acknowledged the pair with a nod, then looked at the victim. 'Can you tell us anything yet?'

'Nothing of any detail until we've completed a more in-depth examination, sir,' Short said. 'Other than to say he was shot at point-blank range. One or two metres.'

Fraser indicated a car parked near the entrance. 'We're going to the Cowgate with Mr Turley,' he said. 'After the PM we'll plot the trajectory of the round that killed him. Soon after that, we should be able to tell which calibre of bullet was used and the make of gun that fired it.'

As Short and Fraser left, Turley spotted the detectives and waved them over.

Close up, Knox saw McGeevor lying prostrate next to an open safe. A small empty cash box lay nearby.

'Afternoon, Alex,' Knox said. Then, motioning to the corpse, he added, 'Not a pleasant sight.'

'No, it isn't, Jack,' Turley said. 'Shot at close range. The bullet entered just below the occipital region. Severed the upper vertebrae and internal carotid artery. Appears to be lodged in the laryngeal prominence – the Adam's apple.'

'Inspector Quinn says a builder at the site next door heard a shot just after one. Would you agree that was when he died?'

Turley nodded. 'Aye, all the indications are that was when stasis began.'

Knox glanced over at Murray, who was taking blood spatter measurements together with his colleague. The forensics officer looked round and acknowledged the others. 'We've done pretty much all we can do at the moment,' he said. 'Including photography and video.'

'Not sure about DNA, though,' Beattie said. 'The only likely contact points are the portacabin door and its handle. Likely to be a lot of cross-contamination.'

'What about the cash box?' Naismith said.

'I don't think the killer touched it, sir,' Murray said. 'Looks like he forced McGeevor to open both safe and cash box.' He waved to the victim. 'Made him hand over the money first.'

'Hmm,' Naismith said. 'So, it would appear the motive was robbery. Do you agree, Jack?'

'I'm sure that's what the killer would like us to think, Alan,' Knox replied. He gestured to the empty cash box. 'I don't think there would have been much in the safe.'

'Likely he paid the weekend's takings into the bank deposit box after closing on Sunday?'

'Probably,' Knox said. 'We've still to talk to his partner, Reynolds. But I'm sure he'll verify.'

'Which means cash wasn't the motive?'

'No,' Knox said. 'I'm thinking about the van connection.'

'Then you think this is Masters' work?'

'Interesting that HOLMES 2 flagged it up.' Knox waved towards the empty cash box. 'And if money isn't the motive, what is?'

DI Quinn approached Turley at that moment and said, 'PC Cullen tells me two of your men are here, sir.'

Turley turned to Naismith. 'We'll be taking the deceased to the Cowgate, Chief Inspector.'

'You're done here?' Naismith said.

'Aye, I think so. The ballistics people will attend the PM to complete their examination. I'll let them do some tests afterward and take possession of the bullet.'

As Turley's assistants entered, everyone departed the portacabin and left them to their task. Murray came over to Knox and said, 'I'll update you if we find any DNA, Jack. But there's something I need to tell you first.'

'Oh, what's that?'

'One of the items of Fairbairn's clothing – a blouse. It's gone astray somewhere in the system. I'm sure we'll find it, but it may cause us a delay in getting further evidence.'

Chapter Fifteen

West Lothian Police had towed their Mobile Incident Unit onto G&S Motors' forecourt just ahead of Scott Reynolds' arrival. Reynolds, a short, bespectacled man in his early forties, exited a silver Audi A6 and approached PC Cullen, who pointed him towards the detectives standing beside Knox's Passat.

Reynolds walked over to Naismith and said, 'You're the Detective Superintendent in charge?'

'Yes,' Naismith replied. 'I take it you're Scott Reynolds, Mr McGeevor's partner?'

'Yes.'

Naismith introduced the others. 'Detective Inspector Knox and Detective Sergeant Fulton. I'm afraid your office is out of bounds at the moment, our forensic people are still in there.' He nodded to the MIU. 'We'll speak to you in the trailer.'

A few minutes later, Reynolds sat opposite Knox and Naismith at a table in the unit. Fulton brought coffees from the dispenser, then took a nearby seat as his colleagues began the interview.

'It's true then,' Reynolds was saying, 'Willie's been shot dead?'

'I'm afraid so,' Naismith replied.

'But why in God's name would anyone want to kill him?'

'We found the safe open and the cash box emptied,' Knox said. 'It appears the gunman forced Mr McGeevor to hand over whatever cash was inside.'

Reynolds shook his head. 'But the killer couldn't have got away with much. Only whatever cash Willie took this morning.'

Naismith nodded. 'You banked your Sunday takings last night?'

'The entire weekend's takings,' Reynolds said. 'Saturday and Sunday. At the bank's deposit machine in Main Street in Broxburn. I can't understand why a thief would wait until today.'

'Is Mr McGeevor always on his own at midday? You go home for lunch?' Knox said.

Reynolds shook his head. 'No, I don't work on a Monday. It's the quietest day of the week.'

'How long have you been in business?' Naismith asked.

Reynolds furrowed his brow. 'Let me think. 2011… no, 2012. Six years.'

'You started as a partnership?'

'Yes. Willie and I have been in the motor trade for over fifteen years. He was with a main Ford van dealer in Edinburgh, I worked at a commercial vehicle garage in Leith. Both of us had built up good contacts in the motor trade, and decided it was time to pool our resources.'

'So, you met McGeevor in the course of business?' Naismith said.

'Aye, we crossed paths two or three times a week. Got on well together.' His face clouded. 'I don't see why anyone would want to murder him.'

'Do you know if he'd made any enemies,' Knox asked. 'Deals that had gone wrong. Arguments he may've had with disgruntled customers, perhaps?'

'No,' Reynolds replied. 'Nothing of that nature. As far as I'm aware, Willie had no enemies. Wasn't that type of person; he was so easy to get along with.'

Naismith nodded. 'Your own relationship,' he said. 'It's always been amicable?'

Reynolds studied Naismith for a long moment, then said, 'We never exchanged a harsh word in all the time I've known him. We trusted each other completely. You have to in this game.'

'What about business transactions,' Knox said. 'You were privy to every deal he made?'

'Not every deal, no,' Reynolds replied. 'Most of our stock we buy from main dealers who take the vehicles as trade-ins. Because we buy upwards of five vans at a time, we can negotiate a rate that allows us a fair resale margin. However, there are other occasions when we may buy privately from someone we know. In such cases, we'll use our own money – not G&S Motors' capital – to purchase a vehicle, and any profit from resale is our own. Willie and I had an agreement on that.'

'So, there's a possibility that McGeevor may have traded a van without it being registered as part of G&S Motors' stock?' Knox asked.

'Uh-huh. Like I say, if he bought it from someone he knew and did the deal out of his own pocket.'

'I'm thinking of one vehicle in particular, a Volkswagen Caddy,' Knox said.

Reynolds raised his eyebrows. 'You know, now that you mention it, I think Willie did buy one about a month ago. White, was it?'

'Yes,' Knox replied. 'You know what happened to it?'

'Hmm,' Reynolds said. 'It was parked at the rear of the forecourt. But only for a few days.'

'He sold it?'

'Must have done. I only recall seeing it there in the early part of the week.'

'He'd have kept a record of who he sold it to?'

Reynolds shrugged. 'I'm not sure. In his own files, maybe. Certainly not in G&S Motors' official stock files.'

Knox mulled over this for a moment. 'Would he have taken it in part exchange for another vehicle?'

'No,' Reynolds said. 'If he had, the sale would have been recorded in the company files. I think it must have been a straight cash transaction, definitely not a part exchange.'

'If he had recorded the deal, where would that file be?'

'Middle drawer of the filing cabinet nearest the desk at the top of the office.' Reynolds shook his head. 'But if it was a private sale, he may not have made a record.' He tapped the side of his nose and added, 'If you get my drift.'

'It would've been off the books?' Knox said.

'Yes.'

'Are there any vehicles which are not part of G&S stock for which McGeevor might have taken the Caddy in part exchange?'

Reynolds nodded. 'Possible. Willie often has the odd couple of vans in his yard at home. He could've done a deal that way. Particularly if he knew the buyer well enough.'

'You've heard of Bluebird Parcel Services?' Naismith said.

'One of the courier firms, isn't it?'

'You've sold vehicles to them?'

'As a company, no. We don't do trade discounts, you see. But we do have a fair number of customers who are drivers doing contract delivery work.'

'Do you know of any who were pally with McGeevor?' Naismith asked.

Reynolds shook his head. 'Not really, no.'

Naismith drained the remainder of his coffee, then said, 'Have either you or McGeevor sold vehicles "off the books" to anyone working as a courier?'

'No,' Reynolds replied emphatically. 'All transactions are dutifully recorded. I keep a kosher set of books,

Detective Chief Inspector. And I go out of my way to keep my nose clean with Customs and Excise and the Inland Revenue.'

* * *

He had reconnoitred the track while delivering a parcel to Howgate the previous week. It was situated on the B7026, four miles the other side of Auchendinny, and cut through a heavily wooded area for a third of a mile, ending at a broad clearing surfaced with bracken and cinder.

It was a half hour before midnight and there was little traffic but as he turned off the road, he cut his lights anyway. He parked the van, set the handbrake, then went to the back and removed two jerrycans. He began by carefully emptying the first over the contents of the back of the van: a large tarpaulin and a dozen wooden crates.

He poured the remaining petrol into the cab, dousing the seats and floor mats, then decanted the rest into the engine bay.

Next, he took a couple of oily rags from a door pocket and lit them with a disposable lighter, then tossed them inside.

Within moments the vehicle burst into flames, which became a raging inferno in less than a minute.

He turned and walked quickly to the road, where his accomplice was waiting.

As he opened the van's passenger door, the driver motioned to the flames, now visible above the treetops, and said, 'Done?'

He nodded. 'Done.'

* * *

More than six hours earlier, the detectives had concluded their interview with Reynolds and were driving back on the M8.

Naismith turned to Knox, who was slowing for traffic merging from a slip road. 'You had a hunch Masters had sold the Caddy to McGeevor?' he said.

'Uh-huh,' Knox replied. 'Lorimer was assaulted by Masters, yet none of the couriers we've interviewed own one. I'd an idea he must've traded it in.'

'Yet Reynolds told us the transaction wasn't on G&S's books?'

'Aye, it's something we'll need to look at,' Knox said.

'Suppose McGeevor had someone "ring" the VW, boss?' Fulton said.

Knox shook his head. 'Not sure I follow, Bill.'

'A trade buyer, say, who gave it a new identity,' Fulton said. 'Came across the practise a lot when I was in Traffic in the nineties. Dodgy dealers in the motor trade would take a stolen car, find an identical model that had been scrapped – same year, same colour – then swap the registration and VIN plates, get a false V5 for the vehicle, then sell it on to an unsuspecting buyer.'

'And as far as the DVLA records are concerned, the legitimate Caddy is still with the last recorded owner?' Knox said.

'Uh-huh. One of hundreds registered in Central Scotland.'

'And without Masters' real name, we haven't a clue who that might be,' Knox said.

'Hmm,' Naismith said. 'And the van McGeevor sold Masters, he doesn't notify the change of ownership right away?'

'The only problem with that,' Fulton said, 'is insurance. Masters would be taking a risk without cover.'

Naismith nodded. 'You're right, Bill,' he said sagely. 'But a risk he's more likely to take in the circumstances.'

Chapter Sixteen

'The DVLA and PNC records show all six of Bluebird's couriers owned their vehicles well in advance of Lorimer's assault and Fairbairn's murder,' Knox was saying. 'What's more, all are insured and none were bought from G&S Motors.'

He and the other detectives were discussing the murder at Broxburn and going over the information gleaned from their interviews.

Naismith marked in McGeevor's name on the whiteboard, and scrawled VW CADDY and OTHER VEHICLE? alongside. 'We know McGeevor disposed of the Caddy,' he said. 'Yet checks with the DVLA show him in possession of another vehicle – a Ford Transit. However, no transfer of ownership has been registered.'

'What if Masters has the Transit garaged somewhere?' Herkiss offered.

'Possible,' Naismith agreed. 'Any other suggestions?'

'Wouldn't McGeevor's wife know if the Transit is still in his possession?' Hathaway said.

Naismith shook his head. 'McGeevor wasn't married, Mark, he lived alone.' He nodded to Knox, and added, 'Jack and I discussed the possibility of the Transit being at his house and asked West Lothian Police to take a look. It isn't there, but that isn't proof he sold it to Masters.' A short pause, then, 'Anyone else?'

'Yes, Alan,' McCann said. 'A bit off topic – Derek Norton's son, Jeff.'

'Aye, what about him?' Naismith asked.

'When Yvonne and I were at Norton's house, his son was in the garden, tinkering with a motorbike. When we told him who we were, his reaction made us suspicious.' McCann looked at her computer. 'With good reason, as it turns out. The machine, a Kawasaki Z900, has been flagged up as stolen.'

'It's on the PNC?' Naismith asked.

McCann nodded. 'Stolen three weeks ago in Colinton Mains Drive, Edinburgh.'

'You got the index number?'

'Not when we left,' McCann replied. 'He'd draped an oily rag over it.' She gave a little smirk. 'When we arrived. Before we told him who we were.'

Naismith grinned. 'Good work, Arlene. You and Yvonne want to pick him up?'

'I'll give his dad a ring first, on the pretence of checking something. Make sure his son's at home,' McCann said.

As McCann went to contact Norton, Knox addressed Hathaway, 'Mark, will you get onto the DVLA and find out how many Volkswagen Caddys are in the East of Scotland? We probably can't check them all, but I'm curious.'

Hathaway nodded and clicked an icon on his computer screen, then the telephone on Knox's desk rang.

He picked up and said, 'DI Knox.'

'Hi,' a voice answered. 'This is Inspector Dave Keller at Penicuik Police Station. The local fire service was called to a track in the woods on the Auchendinny-Leadburn road last night. One of our patrol cars also attended. A van had been torched. Pretty much only a skeleton left, but we still managed to decipher the index number and VIN plate. We checked the PNC and it gave the registered keeper's name and address. It also flagged up your interest.'

'The owner's a William McGeevor? The vehicle's a Ford Transit?' Knox said.

'Aye,' Keller replied. 'Not that you'd be able to tell from what's left of it.'

'Thanks, Dave,' Knox said. 'I'll have a couple of our guys come up and take a look.'

'Fine,' Keller replied. 'It's at the end of a dirt track four miles the other side of Auchendinny.'

Knox ended the call and went to Naismith, who'd just returned to his office. 'The Transit McGeevor sold to Masters, Alan,' he said. 'Penicuik Police have found its burnt-out remains at the end of a track on the Auchendinny-Leadburn Road, fifteen miles south of the city.'

Naismith nodded. 'He's tying up loose ends. Getting rid of anything that might incriminate him.' He paused. 'Worth checking, you think?'

Knox shrugged. 'Penicuik Police tell me there's nothing but a shell. It wouldn't do any harm, though. I'll send Bill and Gary to take a look.'

* * *

The Kawasaki was gone from the garden when McCann and Mason returned to 6 Cochrane Terrace. Norton's wife, a dumpy woman with greying hair tied in a bun, answered the door. 'Yes?' she said.

'Mrs Norton?'

'Uh-huh.'

'We're the police officers who called earlier,' McCann said. 'We asked to speak to your son, Jeff.'

'Oh, yes,' she said. 'You spoke to my husband again today. On the phone?'

'That's right,' McCann replied. 'Mr Norton said he'd be home for his lunch and probably wouldn't be here when we arrived. We explained it was Jeff we wanted to see.'

Mrs Norton shook her head. 'Jeff's not here.'

'Really?' McCann said. 'His father said he was.'

'When you phoned, yes,' Ms Norton said. 'He went out soon afterward.'

'Did his father tell him we were coming?' Mason asked.

Mrs Norton shrugged. 'I honestly don't know. He might have.'

'Did he take his motorbike with him?'

'Yes.'

'Did he say where he was going?'

'No, he left without saying anything.'

'Have you any idea where he's likely to have gone?'

Mrs Norton pursed her lips. 'I couldn't say for sure.' She placed a finger on her chin, thought for a moment, then added, 'Sometimes he and his biker pals hang out at Joe's Café.'

'Joe's Café?'

'Yes,' Mrs Norton said. 'It's in Dalkeith Country Park. I think it's run by the Town Council.'

McCann thanked her and left, then she and Mason got back in the car.

'Dalkeith Country Park?' McCann said.

Mason activated the sat nav. 'I think it's on the A6094 on the fringes of Dalkeith,' she said, then after consulting the device, added, 'I was right. The entrance is at the eastern end of the High Street.'

'How far is it from here?' McCann asked.

'Only a ten-minute drive.'

The detectives found Dalkeith Country Park situated just off the Dalkeith-Musselburgh road, its entrance clearly marked. Mason stopped and studied a "You Are Here" signpost, which gave the location of each of the park's attractions.

Joe's Café was near a small boating lake, next to which was a car park. The café was a rustic-style cabin positioned alongside a grove of trees, which served hot rolls, sandwiches and drinks from a hatch to customers who sat at tables outside.

As Mason drove the Vectra into one of the allotted spaces, she and McCann saw four motorcycles parked nearby, one of which was the stolen Kawasaki. McCann inclined her head towards the machine and Mason nodded. The women walked to the café, then McCann spotted Norton sitting at a table shaded by a large oak tree. She nudged Mason and said, 'Over there.'

Mason gave a nod of acknowledgement. 'His mother was right,' she whispered, 'he is with his biker pals.'

The pair approached the table where Norton sat with three men around his own age, late teens or early twenties. Like Norton, they wore biker leathers, the jackets adorned with an assortment of patches and stickers.

Their table was littered with empty soft drink bottles and polystyrene cups, suggesting that one or two of them had been there for some time. The area echoed to their loud banter, interspersed occasionally with raucous laughter.

As McCann drew near, Norton was sitting with his back to the detectives, and hadn't seen their approach.

She tapped Norton's shoulder and said, 'Jeff Norton?'

Norton reacted as if McCann had laid a red-hot poker on his shoulder. He jumped to his feet and turned on her, a look of rage on his face. 'What the fuck do you want?' he said.

'Jeff Norton,' McCann continued, 'you're under arrest for the theft of a Kawasaki motorcycle taken from the garden of a house at 18 Colinton Mains View on the seventeenth of January this year. You don't have to say–'

Norton didn't wait for the remainder of the caution. He drew back his arm and aimed a blow at McCann's head. The officer dodged left as Norton followed through, then grabbed his wrist and swung his arm in a 90-degree arc.

Norton's momentum did the rest: he executed an almost complete somersault, landing on his back. McCann continued holding his wrist, which she twisted forcefully. Norton screamed as the movement made him turn and face the ground. Then the officer thrust his arm behind his back and removed a pair of handcuffs from her waistband. She slipped one manacle over his right hand, repeated the process with his left, then closed the cuffs with a resounding *snap*.

Her adversary's mates, meanwhile, hadn't moved an inch: they looked on open-mouthed as Mason helped her colleague raise Norton to his feet.

Norton appeared winded by his fall; all the fight had gone out of him. He stood unsteadily, looking both dazed and bewildered.

Only then did one of his mates react. The smallest of the group, a spotty-faced teenager with dark curly hair, said, 'Hey! That's police brutality, that is.'

McCann's free hand went to her waistband for a second time. She removed an expandable truncheon, flicked it into its extended position, then waved it at the young man. 'So far, your friend here's the only one we're interested in,' she said. 'He's being arrested on three charges. Theft, attempted assault on a police officer, and resisting arrest. But if you or any of your mates want to accompany him, we'll be happy to accommodate you.'

As McCann spoke, Mason had a two-way radio in her hand and was saying, 'This is DC Mason requesting backup from local police. Two officers making an arrest at Joe's Café, Dalkeith Country Park.'

A moment later, a crackled response came over the radio. "Message received. Priority given for immediate response."

A tall youth seated next to the one who had spoken raised his hands, palms outwards. 'You'll get no trouble from me, missus,' he said to McCann.

The freckle-faced teenager on his right nodded. 'Nor me.'

At this, the curly-haired young man who'd been the first to speak shrugged and shook his head. 'I don't want any bother, either.'

* * *

'Nothing but a charred lump of tin,' Fulton was saying. He and Herkiss had returned to Gayfield Square from Auchendinny after inspecting the burned-out Ford Transit and were speaking to Knox.

'Absolutely trashed,' Herkiss agreed. 'Everything. All the electricals, tyres. Nothing's recognisable. Must've used at least a couple of gallons of petrol. Only one of the registration plates was decipherable, but only just.'

'It's like the DCI said,' Knox replied. 'He's tying up loose ends.'

'Begs the question, though, boss,' Fulton said. 'If the other six couriers still have transport, where does Masters fit in? Has he really anything to do with this Bluebird outfit?'

Knox shrugged. 'Murray's tyre prints point to a connection, Bill. The only Byrona tyres in Scotland were sold to Bluebird and the two independents we've already checked out.'

'What about Masters running two vans? The DCI agreed it was feasible,' Herkiss said.

'Yes, Alan did say that, Gary. And I agree it's likely. I've a gut feeling, though, that there's an element we're not seeing yet.'

Hathaway left his desk and jerked his thumb towards his computer. 'The VW Caddys you asked me to take a look at, boss?'

'Aye, Mark. What did you find out?'

'One hundred and eighty-seven white models are registered in East Central Scotland. Four hundred and forty-nine if you take in Strathclyde and the west.'

'Hmm,' Knox said. 'Thought as much. Bit of a mountain to climb if we have to sift through that lot.' He shook his head. 'What we need now is for something else to surface.'

Mason and McCann walked into the office at that moment and Knox changed tack. 'You ladies get a result?' he said.

Mason grinned. 'Not without a struggle,' she said. 'But, yes, Jeff Norton's in custody at Dalkeith Police Station. And the stolen motorbike's been recovered.'

'He resisted arrest?' Knox said.

Mason nodded. 'Threw a punch at Arlene. But she dodged it and had him in cuffs in seconds. I've never seen anyone move so fast.'

McCann shrugged, playing it down. 'Relatively tame, really. Compared to some hard cases I helped to collar as a PC on Saturday nights in Glasgow.'

Knox smiled. 'Good work, anyway. A wee highlight at last.'

'Nothing breaking with the Fairbairn murder, boss?' Mason said.

Knox shook his head. 'Not much.'

The door opened again and DI Murray and DS Beattie entered. Knox was encouraged to see the forensics officers were smiling.

'Good news, Ed?' he asked Murray.

'Mixed,' Murray replied. 'I checked out McGeevor's files at G&S Motors' premises. No record of who he sold the Caddy to. No record of him selling the Transit either – though I gather that's academic now. The van's been torched?'

'Aye, Masters set it aflame after drowning it in petrol last night at some woods near Auchendinny,' Knox replied.

Knox gestured to the file Murray had under his arm. 'You look as if you may have some good news,' he said. 'The DNA results are in?'

Murray nodded. 'First off, we're still waiting on the analysis of the blouse. But the good news is they've found it. And, aye, the DNA results are in. Negative on Mackenzie and Norton. Positive on Smeaton.'

Knox's face lit up. 'Ryan Smeaton's our man?'

'Like I told you, mixed results. His test came in positive – but only for familial DNA,' Murray said.

'Familial DNA?'

'Aye, Jack,' Murray said. 'The DNA markers indicate a close match, but not a complete one. Which indicates the killer is related to Smeaton. Either a parent or a sibling.'

Fulton scratched his head. 'Really?' he said. 'How does that work?'

'It's all to do with genetic make-up, Bill,' Beattie explained. 'Each string of DNA has particular markers. One of these is on the Y-chromosome. It's only shared by fathers, sons and brothers.'

'So, Smeaton's likely to be Masters' brother?' Knox said.

Murray nodded. 'Yes.'

Knox glanced at his watch. 'Okay, it's three-thirty. Smeaton should be at home.' He turned to Hathaway. 'Mark, get onto Livingston Police, will you? Ask them to go to 20 Clover Way. Tell them to inform Smeaton something important's come up and we want to see him here. Tell them we need his cooperation and they've to bring him in now.'

'They're to arrest him?'

'No,' Knox replied. 'Not at this point. Impress on them the need to be subtle. It's only a request at this point. On the other hand, they've to make the implication clear: if he doesn't come willingly, arrest is the alternative.'

Chapter Seventeen

'I don't understand why you want to speak to me again,' Smeaton was saying. 'I thought we covered everything when I talked to you at home.'

Smeaton was in one of Gayfield Square Police Station's three interview rooms. Seated at the table opposite him were Knox and Fulton. Naismith was in the room next door, viewing the exchange on a closed-circuit television monitor.

Knox studied the ex-paratrooper. A fine sheen of sweat had formed on his forehead and it was evident he was uncomfortable.

'There's been a development,' Knox said, 'with the result of your DNA test.'

Smeaton regarded Knox with a look of hostility. 'Which implicates me?'

'Not directly, no,' Knox replied. 'But our forensic team tell us your DNA specimen flagged up a family connection.'

'I don't understand,' Smeaton said.

'Markers in the Y-chromosome indicate the man we are looking for is either your father or your brother. I think the latter's more likely, so I'd like to ask about your siblings. Can you tell us about them?'

Smeaton said nothing for a long moment, then shook his head. 'My natural mother,' he said, 'had some sort of mental breakdown when I was nine years old. My brother and I were taken into care.'

'Where was this?'

'The place where we were born,' Smeaton replied. 'Camelon, near Falkirk.'

'What happened to your mother, exactly?' Knox asked.

'My father – I don't remember him – left her when I was seven and my brother was four. She had a nervous breakdown, followed by bouts of depression. We were at home on our own for long periods of time. The council's social work department heard about it and got a court order. We were taken into care.'

'Uh-huh,' Knox said. 'What was your father's name?'

'Gaffney,' Smeaton said. 'Thomas Gaffney. I was fostered at the age of fourteen. Smeaton's my foster parents' name.'

'And your brother?'

'He was fostered a year before me. When he was ten, I think.'

'What is your brother's Christian name?'

'Jack,' Smeaton said. 'Jack Gaffney.'

'What is his foster parents' surname?'

Smeaton shrugged. 'I don't know,' he replied. 'The people at the care home would only tell me he was fostered by a couple in St Andrews. I never found out their address.'

'You weren't curious?' Fulton said.

Smeaton nodded. 'Of course I was curious. The care home people told me the foster parents didn't want me to know.'

'When was the last time you saw your brother?' Knox said.

'I told you. At the care home, when I was thirteen and he was ten.'

'You haven't communicated with him since?'

'Only once. My foster parents live here in Edinburgh. After I joined the army, Sheila – that's my foster mother – got in touch with the home and asked them to forward my contact details to Jack's foster parents, but she never received a reply.'

Smeaton shook his head and went on, 'We weren't particularly close, really. Not even at the care home. Three years is a big difference when you're that age. We didn't have that much in common.'

'So, you haven't seen your brother in sixteen years?' Knox asked.

'That's right,' Smeaton said. 'As I said, I was in the army between the ages of eighteen and twenty-five. I met Linda, got married, and soon afterward we moved to Livingston. I didn't try to contact him again and he didn't contact me. It could have something to do with family history. I guess his childhood memories may have traumatised him in some way.'

'What happened to your mother?' Knox asked.

Smeaton shrugged. 'Suicide. She took an overdose of pills back in 2005.'

'This care home you went to, it's in Falkirk?'

'Yes. 18 Dundrennan Drive.'

'Okay, Ryan,' Knox said. 'We'll have to check out everything you've told us. However, I'd like to impress on you the seriousness of the situation. It's almost one hundred per cent likely your brother has committed murder. If you should see him, or if he should try to contact you, you must let us know. Do you understand?'

Smeaton nodded. 'I understand,' he said.

Knox rose from the desk and indicated the door. 'Right,' he said. 'You can go. See Sergeant Rogers on the desk and he'll have an officer drive you home.' Knox held Smeaton's gaze and added, 'But bear in mind, if there's anything we have to verify, we'll need to speak to you again.'

* * *

'What do you think, Jack?' Naismith said. Knox and Fulton had joined the DCI in the adjoining interview room soon after Smeaton left.

Knox shook his head. 'I have the feeling he's lying,' he replied. 'I find it hard to believe anyone fostering a ten-year-old boy would deny his brother access.'

'And when they became adults,' Naismith said, 'surely one or the other would have tried to make contact?'

'I thought it odd, too, that at one point in the interview Smeaton said his brother may have been traumatised,' Fulton said. 'I got the feeling he was hiding something.'

'Well, I daresay we'll find out before long,' Naismith said, then glanced at his watch. 'Right, we'd better get onto this care home, Jack. See if we can track down his foster parents before we call it a day.'

Knox looked at his partner. 'Bill's just about to give them a ring, Alan.' He took his phone from his pocket and added, 'Meanwhile, I've just had a text message from DI June Short, the ballistics officer we spoke to in Bathgate. She wants to update me on their findings.'

Naismith nodded in acknowledgement, then he and Fulton left the room.

Knox highlighted Short's number, pressed *call*, and a moment later a voice answered.

'DI June Short.'

'Hi, June. It's Jack Knox. You asked me to ring you?'

'Ah yes, Jack,' Short said. 'We've got the results of the ballistics tests.'

'Uh-huh,' Knox said.

'The killer fired at an almost forty-five-degree angle, which means he had to have been standing over McGeevor when he pulled the trigger.'

'Yes,' Knox said. 'That confirms what you told me at Broxburn.'

'It does,' Short said. 'But the bullet Mr Turley took from the deceased is a 9x19mm Parabellum round, which indicates it was fired from an automatic pistol.'

'And?'

'We've studied the rifling and we're almost sure it came from an Austrian-made Glock. More specifically, a Glock 17.'

'That has significance?'

'Yes,' Short said. 'In the UK, Glock 17s are almost exclusively an army weapon. Issued to special forces: the SAS, SBS and the Parachute Regiment.'

Chapter Eighteen

Fulton's call to Falkirk's Glenlee Care Home at Dundrenann Drive reached the duty supervisor, who revealed that Jack Gaffney had been fostered by a Mr Archie Grant and his wife Elsie, who resided at 17 Ochiltree Crescent, St Andrews.

Knox had updated Naismith on DI June Short's findings before winding up on Tuesday evening, and the following morning he and his partner were headed north.

As they crossed the Firth of Forth via the new Queensferry Crossing, Fulton said, 'I overheard Naismith telling Yvonne that Gartcosh wanted to interview her about Reilly?'

'Yes, the DCI told me before we left,' Knox said. 'Apparently, he appealed. They're holding a tribunal at eleven-thirty this morning. Because Naismith enacted the suspension, they want him to be present.'

'A tribunal?'

'Aye,' Knox replied. 'Three chief superintendents and two chief inspectors. Apparently, one of the latter will represent Reilly, the other Yvonne.'

Fulton shook his head. 'Surely, Reilly hasn't a leg to stand on?'

Knox shrugged. 'I wouldn't bet on it. Naismith told me Reilly's still able to pull a string or two. He's in the habit of shaking hands with the right people, apparently.'

'Mm-hmm,' Fulton said. 'He's a Mason.'

Knox entered Fife and took the coastal route via Kirkaldy, Leven and Anstruther, arriving at St Andrews just before eleven.

17 Ochiltree Crescent was a compact, semi-detached bungalow on a new-build estate situated a mile east of the world-famous Royal and Ancient Golf Club. As Knox drew to a halt, he saw a middle-aged man and woman tending a flowerbed. The detectives exited the car, then the woman looked over. 'You're the policemen who called earlier?' she said.

Knox and Fulton introduced themselves, then Mrs Grant gestured to the door. 'Please, go in,' she said. She took off her gardening gloves, then laid down a pair of secateurs and motioned to her husband. 'Archie, will you put these gardening things in the shed and come back inside?'

'Yes, dear,' her husband replied. 'I'll be there in a moment.'

A minute or two later, the detectives were seated on a pair of beige armchairs in the living room while the Grants sat on a matching settee opposite. Mrs Grant offered to make the detectives tea but Knox thanked her and declined. 'We left the office early this morning and stopped off at Anstruther for breakfast,' he explained.

Mrs Grant looked disappointed. 'Oh, I see,' she said. 'I would've been happy to have put the kettle on.'

There was a short silence, then Mr Grant said, 'Glenlee Care Home gave you Elsie's details?'

'Yes,' Knox said. 'We wanted to ask about Jack Gaffney. They told us Jack had been fostered to a Mr and Mrs Grant.'

Mrs Grant glanced at her husband and said, 'Jack came to us before I married Archie. He came to live with me and my then husband, Don, in 2002. They seem to have updated their records with Archie's name. Sorry about the confusion.'

'I see,' Knox said, then continued, 'Were you and your former husband aware Jack had a brother at Glenlee?'

'Yes,' Mrs Grant said. 'Ryan. He was three years older.'

Knox nodded, then said, 'After you fostered Jack, did anyone at the home contact you to ask if Ryan could visit his brother?'

'The supervisor told us it would be in Ryan's best interest if he didn't see Jack for a while, to get him used to the separation,' Mrs Grant said. 'Don and I thought it was a cruel stance to take, but he assured us it was in the children's interest.'

'Glenlee didn't allow Ryan to phone his brother either?'

'Uh-huh.' Mrs Grant shrugged. 'Don and I thought it strange, but went along with it.'

'Was Jack able to contact his brother at any point?'

'Jack kept asking about Ryan, so six months after he came to live with us, I got in touch with the supervisor again. He told me Ryan didn't want to see Jack, or talk to him. To be honest, I found it hard to believe.' She shook her head. 'But then I remembered the boy's background and that his mother had a mental illness. I guessed it might have affected the boy.'

'And Jack?' Knox said. 'He came to terms with it?'

'Eventually,' Mrs Grant said. 'It took a while, though.'

'How long was he with you?'

'Eight years,' Mrs Grant replied. 'He completed a course in media studies at Napier University in Edinburgh when he was eighteen. He shared a flat with other students to begin with, visiting Don and I at the weekends. Then he got a job with a public relations firm and rented his own flat. When Don died of lung cancer in 2012, Jack stopped visiting. I don't think he could bear coming back to the house where he'd spent so much of his childhood. He just doted on Don.'

'What kind of personality did he have?' Knox asked.

'As a child?' Mrs Grant said. 'Quiet in the beginning. A bit withdrawn. Soon after he came to us and started making friends, he came out of his shell. By the time he grew into his teens he was outgoing, full of confidence. To be honest, though, he was still prone to mood swings.'

'When did you last see him?' Knox asked.

'Six years ago,' Mrs Grant replied. 'At my former husband's funeral.'

'Does he ever phone?' Fulton asked.

'No, never. I don't hear from him at all these days. Not even a Christmas card.'

'Have you ever heard of a John Masters?' Knox asked.

Mrs Grant frowned. 'No,' she said. 'Why?'

Knox shook his head. 'It's not important,' he replied. 'Do you happen to have Jack's address?'

'No, I'm afraid not. The last I heard – that would be around the time Don died – he was still in his flat in Gorgie.'

'What, was he still with the public relations company?'

'No, he told me at Don's funeral that he'd started his own business. Some kind of delivery service.'

'He was a courier?' Knox asked. 'Delivering parcels?'

Mrs Grant nodded. 'What was his firm's name?'

Her brow furrowed as she searched her memory. 'Something to do with a colour. Green... no, blue-something.'

'Bluebird Parcel Services?'

'Yes, that's it.' She studied Knox for a long moment. 'Has Donald done something serious?'

Knox raised his eyebrows. 'Donald?'

'Yes,' Mrs Grant said. 'Sorry, I thought you knew. After Jack left us, he took my ex-husband's Christian name and surname. He told me at Don's funeral he'd changed it by deed poll.'

'What is your ex-husband's surname?' Knox said.

'Russell,' Mrs Grant replied. 'Don Russell.'

* * *

Gartcosh Scottish Crime Campus was situated near the M73, eight miles north-east of Glasgow. The new Police Scotland headquarters opened in 2014, designed from scratch to incorporate five key law enforcement agencies: Organised Crime, Drugs, Revenue and Customs, Procurator Fiscal Services and Forensics.

Y-Shaped after the Y-chromosome, the four-storey building was created as a state-of-the-art facility and covered 12,600 square meters of real estate, with masonry of varying widths repeated around the façade, designed to replicate the sequences of male and female DNA.

Naismith left his Volvo xc60 at the adjacent car park, then he and Mason went into a central atrium where they were greeted by a civilian receptionist.

'Good morning,' she said. 'Do you have an appointment?'

'Yes,' Naismith replied. 'Detective Chief Inspector Naismith and Detective Constable Mason. We're here to see Chief Superintendent Mullin at eleven-thirty.'

The receptionist nodded. 'May I see your warrant cards, please?'

Naismith and Mason handed over their ID cards, which the woman checked. She glanced at a desktop computer, scrolled through a list on the screen, and said, 'Ah, here we are. Detective Chief Superintendent Mullin. Room 201b, fourth floor.'

She handed back their cards and waved to a pair of lifts situated near the foot of a sweeping staircase. 'Take one of the lifts to the fourth floor, 201b is to your left.'

Naismith turned to Mason on exiting the lift and said, 'Mullin will chair the tribunal. I've had dealings with him before. He's a fair man.'

They continued along the corridor and found 201b, where Naismith's knock was answered by a man wearing a chief inspector's uniform. He smiled and said, 'DCI Naismith and DC Mason?'

Naismith nodded. 'Yes.'

'Chief Inspector Brian Forsyth,' he said, then shook their hands. 'I'll be representing you at the hearing.' He waved them into a large room whose predominant feature was a substantial-looking wooden table behind which three chairs had been arranged. A further two were positioned at right angles on the left, and three others in the centre faced the table at a distance of five feet.

Forsyth looked at his watch. '11.25am,' he said. 'The others should be here soon. My opposite number, DCI George Laidlaw, is representing DI Reilly.'

'Who are the other officers on the panel?' Naismith asked.

'Chief Superintendent Dave Ramsey and Chief Superintendent Nigel McCrone,' Forsyth replied. 'Chief Superintendent Mullin is Chair.'

'Yes, I was told that earlier,' Naismith said.

'I've studied your report as the basis of the case against DI Reilly, Chief Inspector,' Forsyth said. 'What you overheard him say to DI Knox, and the insubordinate comments he made against you. There's nothing you wish to add or amend?'

'No,' Naismith said. 'I put in my report exactly what happened.'

Then the door opened and five others entered the room. The three senior officers took their seats behind the table while the other two, DCI Laidlaw and DI Reilly, went to the seats on the left.

Chief Superintendent Mullin, a stocky man with a thick moustache, waved to the chairs opposite and nodded to Forsyth, Naismith and Mason. 'Please,' he said, 'take a seat.'

He continued, 'My name is Chief Superintendent Bill Mullin and I'll be chairing the tribunal today.' He motioned to his companions and added, 'The other officers present are Chief Superintendent Dave Ramsey, seated on my left, and Chief Superintendent Nigel

McCrone, seated on my right. Detective Chief Inspector George Laidlaw will represent Detective Inspector Reilly.'

Mullin leafed through a folder on the desk in front of him and continued, 'Okay, let's get started. The purpose of this tribunal is to determine the fairness of Detective Inspector Reilly's dismissal from an active murder inquiry on 13 August and the pending disciplinary action. The charges are insubordination and attempting to bring into disrepute the reputation of a fellow officer, DC Yvonne Mason.' He looked at Laidlaw. 'DCI Laidlaw, will you confirm that DI Reilly is appealing these charges?'

'Yes, sir, he is.'

Mullin studied Laidlaw for a long moment. 'DI Reilly is denying that DCI Naismith overheard him admit to another officer he had set a trap for DC Mason? That he used a mobile telephone confiscated from a drugs offender to make an emergency 999 call? That he told the operator DC Mason was driving in a manner likely to endanger other road users?'

'DI Reilly feels the facts, as they are presented, paint him in a poor light, sir,' Laidlaw said.

'How, specifically?' Mullin asked.

'With respect, sir, DI Reilly thinks DCI Naismith may not have represented the exchange between him and DI Knox exactly as it occurred,' Laidlaw said. 'The DCI only *heard* the conversation. He didn't see the interaction between DI Knox and himself. The DCI was in, ahem, a toilet cubicle at the time.'

'I'm aware of that. Go on,' Mullin said.

'DI Knox confronted DI Reilly and acted aggressively towards him. DI Reilly was at pains to point out that he had only been doing his duty in reporting DC Mason.'

'Is DI Reilly telling us he didn't say DI Mason was weaving all over the road?' Mullin said. 'We have a recording of the 999 call.'

'No, sir, he isn't. He insists that at one point she was driving in such a manner.'

Mullin motioned to Reilly. 'And just how did he come to be at Holyrood Park Road when DC Mason left DI Knox's flat? He was registered at the Crowne Plaza Hotel on Royal Terrace. That's a good four miles distant, is it not?'

'Yes, sir, it is,' Laidlaw said. 'The reason for DI Reilly being there is that he had overheard DI Knox talking to his partner, DS Fulton a day or two earlier. They were discussing keeping fit. He heard Knox tell Fulton about his morning jog from Holyrood Park Road. It starts at the eastern end of Hunter's bog, a long valley behind Salisbury Crags, then completes a circuit that takes in the ruin of St Anthony's Chapel overlooking St Margaret's Loch. From there, it joins the Radical Road, a cliffside path that winds back to the start point. The route affords a panoramic view of the city.

'DI Reilly also liked to keep fit and thought it a good idea. In fact, he had completed the run and was getting back into his car in Holyrood Park Road when he saw DC Mason's Mini.'

Mullin glanced at Mason. 'DC Mason,' he said, 'is there a possibility that DI Reilly may have gone back to his car after such a run on 13 August?' He waved in her direction. 'You may address the Chair.'

Mason shook her head. 'No, sir. It is my belief that DI Reilly deliberately chose to be there that morning. I don't think he'd undertaken the run.'

'I see,' Mullin said. 'Please tell us why.'

'Thank you, sir,' Mason said. 'On Sunday, 12 August, we had almost completed our shift and were all assembled in the MI room at Gayfield Square. I was in the process of moving a bag of shopping near my desk when DS McCann, who was seated alongside me, saw it contained two bottles of spirits. She commented in a joking fashion, and I explained I was taking them to DI Knox's flat that evening. It was his birthday on Monday. I told her we intended to have a celebratory drink.

'When I moved the bag, DI Reilly, who was sitting at an adjacent desk, heard the clink of glass. I believe he followed me to DI Knox's flat on Sunday evening and returned on Monday with the intention of making the call. He guessed I might be on or near the limit, and of course he was right.'

'Hmm,' Mullin said, then glanced at Reilly. 'DI Reilly, I'm concerned about the mobile phone you used to make the call – how do you explain that?'

'DI Reilly–' Laidlaw said.

Mullin waved the DCI into silence. 'No, DCI Laidlaw, I want to hear from DI Reilly himself. He may address the Chair.'

Reilly shuffled in his seat, gave Mullin a disconcerted look, then said, 'I don't deny I had the phone, sir,' he said. 'When I got back in the car after my run, I saw DC Mason leave East Parkside and begin driving erratically. I was wearing jogging gear and had left my smartphone in my suit pocket back at the hotel. It was then I remembered the phone in the glovebox.'

Mullin shook his head. 'You're aware confiscated items should be handed in when an operation is ended?'

'Yes, sir. I'm sorry. I'd forgotten.'

Mullin studied Reilly for a long moment, then said, 'Yet you boasted of its existence when you spoke to DI Knox. That it was, quote, "Virtually untraceable".'

'I'm sorry, sir,' Reilly said. 'I was reacting to the threatening way in which DI Knox had confronted me.'

'And your derogatory comments about DCI Naismith? That he was wrong in assigning the Fairbairn murder case to Knox? That it was your belief that you were more qualified to lead the investigation? You also disagreed with his policy on how officers address one another?'

'I was expressing an opinion to DI Knox,' Reilly said. 'I don't want to sound arrogant, sir, but I could have led the Longniddry murder inquiry, and done so efficiently. I think my homicide clear-up record for this year alone reflects that.' He paused for a moment and added, 'With respect to DCI Naismith, I think there was an element of favouritism in DI Knox's appointment.'

'Really?' Mullin said. 'And how do you arrive at that conclusion?'

'At the start of the investigation, I interviewed Ms Shona Kirkbride, the girl who was with Ms Fairbairn on the night of her murder,' Reilly replied. 'She told me the man with the murder suspect was a Mr Joe Turner. As I had elicited this information, I felt I should be the one to see Turner in the subsequent interview. But DCI Naismith passed me over in favour of DI Knox.'

Mullin looked over at Forsyth. 'Is that recorded in DCI Naismith's report?'

Forsyth took a moment to riffle through Naismith's file, then shook his head. 'No, sir. It doesn't appear to be.'

Mullin gestured to Naismith. 'DCI Naismith,' he said. 'Why did you assign the Fairbairn murder case to DI Knox?'

The DCI looked at Reilly. 'Certainly not because of any favouritism, sir. I explained at the outset I thought both DI Reilly and DI Knox were equally qualified to lead the investigation. I didn't discount DI Reilly's abilities. However, DI Knox had the advantage of local knowledge, and I believed that would be key to solving the case. I still do.'

'And DI Reilly's specific claim that he was passed over when you gave the Turner interview to DI Knox?'

'I was at pains to point out to him that we were working as a team.' Naismith shook his head. 'If you'll forgive me, sir. I think when I made the decision to appoint DI Knox as lead investigator, DI Reilly ceased to be a team player.'

'Hmm.' Mullin gave Reilly a withering look. 'Which leaves us, DI Reilly, with your comment that you felt DCI Naismith's attitude to discipline was lacking. You told DI

Knox you believed officers calling each other by their Christian names was wrong?'

'Yes, sir. I think discipline is one of the most important elements in policing. I was trained to respect rank, and feel the best results in man-management are achieved by maintaining this formality. I would quote the old saying, "familiarity breeds contempt". I think DCI Naismith's approach can only lead to a breakdown in discipline,' Reilly said.

Mullin glanced at the senior officers seated with him. 'Do other members of the panel have questions for the appellant or other officers in the case?'

Ramsey and McCrone shook their heads, then Mullin closed the file. 'Very well,' he said, 'myself and other members of this panel will now deliberate. Both parties will have our decision within forty-eight hours. This tribunal is closed. You may go.'

Chapter Nineteen

The Eurowings Airbus A320 banked and held to the south shoreline of the Forth estuary as it made its approach to Edinburgh Airport. The aircraft had departed Stuttgart at 06.50 and was on schedule for its stated arrival time of 10.50.

Lena Weber and Imke Fischer, two of the aircraft's 178 passengers, exchanged glances as the plane swooped low and the girls spotted the first of the three bridges spanning the river.

'Look!' Fischer said. 'The Forth Rail Bridge.'

Weber smiled. 'I can see the other two also,' she said. 'The weather is so nice here today.'

Fischer grimaced. 'Unlike our visit last year,' she said. 'It rained on the first three days.'

Her petite blonde companion nodded. The two had first visited Scotland the previous year, having fallen in love with the country after seeing *Outlander* on German television. The series was broadcast on the RTL Passion network and had been a nationwide hit. Like many of their countrymen, Weber and Fischer were captivated by the tale of a post-World War II English nurse who had travelled back in time to eighteenth-century Scotland.

On their last trip, the girls had visited Glencoe, Kinloch Rannoch and Doune Castle, where many of the first episodes of the series had been filmed. As staunch fans, this time the girls planned to visit locations in Edinburgh and southern Scotland, beginning with Drumlanrig Castle in Dumfries and Galloway.

Although they'd saved for their five-day break, their budget was limited, so the pair decided to ease their finances by staying in a youth hostel in central Edinburgh, and to hitch-hike whenever possible.

After their plane landed, the girls caught an express coach to Waverley Bridge, then walked the short distance via Princes Street and North Bridge to their hostel in Niddry Street. Soon they had booked in, taken lunch in the hostel canteen, then walked to nearby South Bridge and boarded a 47 bus.

They arrived in Penicuik shortly after 2pm, crossed John Street to the A766 Carlops Road and extended their thumbs. They had only a short wait before an articulated lorry drew to a halt. The girls caught up with the vehicle and Weber opened the cab door.

The driver leaned over and said, 'Where're you headed, ladies?'

'Thornhill,' Weber said. 'It's near the A76.'

The driver nodded. 'I can take you as far as Abington, where the B797 branches off. It connects with the A76 twenty or so miles farther on. It's likely someone'll give you a lift from there.'

Fischer, a hazel-eyed brunette in her late teens, smiled. 'Thank you,' she said. 'That is very kind.'

The girls clambered into the cab carrying lightweight rucksacks. Any unnecessary gear had been left at the hostel, exchanged for packets of sandwiches and bottles of mineral water.

The driver, a grey-haired man in his early fifties, put the vehicle in gear and moved off. 'So,' he said, 'why are you headed to Thornhill?'

'We are going to Drumlanrig Castle,' Fischer said. 'You have heard of it?'

The driver shook his head. 'Can't say I have. Bit off the beaten track?'

Fischer gave him a mystified look. 'Sorry,' she said, 'my English is not so good. I do not understand "off the beaten track".'

The driver grinned. 'It's a saying,' he explained. 'Off a side road, perhaps. Somewhere not too well known.'

Fischer nodded. 'Yes,' she said. 'I am thinking so. Maybe it is not well known.'

'It is a beautiful castle where part of *Outlander* was filmed. It features in an episode called "Vengeance is mine",' Weber said.

The driver gave a comprehending nod. 'Ah,' he said. 'I see, *Outlander*. The television series based on the books by Diana Gabaldon. My wife and daughter are fans. They've seen all the shows. My wife's read all the books, too.'

'Yes,' Weber said. 'We are fans also.'

'The programme's popular in Germany? I take it that's where you're from?'

'Yes,' Fischer said. 'The programme is very popular in Germany. And we're from Wangen. It is a district of Stuttgart.'

'Stuttgart? That's southern Germany, isn't it?'

'Yes,' Weber said. 'Baden-Württemberg, south east. You have visited?'

The driver shook his head. 'No,' he said. 'My wife, my daughter and I have been to Switzerland, though. Interlaken.'

'Ah, yes,' Fischer said. 'That is not so far from us.'

'So, what do you girls do in Stuttgart?'

'You mean work?' Fischer replied.

The driver nodded. 'Yes.'

Fischer shrugged. 'We're part of the sales staff in a department store called Müller.'

The driver smiled. 'Nice to get away for a wee while, eh?'

Both girls laughed, then Fischer said, 'Yes, very nice.'

* * *

'Smeaton told us a complete pack of lies,' Fulton was saying. He and Knox were on the outskirts of St Andrews, heading back to Edinburgh.

'What worries me is the gun used to kill McGeevor,' Knox replied. 'Smeaton's ex-para. I'm positive the weapon's his.'

'They've got to be in cahoots,' Fulton said. 'If that's where he got the gun.'

Knox nodded, then keyed a number into his mobile's hands-free unit. A dialling tone came through the car's speakers and there was a brief clicking sound, then Hathaway answered: 'Hi, boss.'

'Mark,' Knox said. 'We've interviewed the Grants at St Andrews. Gaffney's real name is Russell.'

'Russell... he's the killer?'

'Yes,' Knox replied. 'We need to arrest him and his brother, Ryan. But here's the thing: I'm convinced the weapon used to kill McGeevor is Smeaton's. Glock 17s are issued to UK special forces, and he's ex-para. For that reason, I want you to proceed with caution. Take Yvonne with you and collar Russell, and ask Arlene and Gary to go for his brother. First, though, I want you to contact Armed Response. Have an ARV unit precede each arrest, just in case. Understand?'

'Yes, boss.'

'And Mark?'

'Aye, boss?'

'Update DCI Naismith, will you?'

'Yes, boss.'

Knox ended the call, and a moment later the phone rang. Knox keyed *accept* and DI Murray's voice came through the speakers. They crackled, the signal breaking up.

'Jack?' he said.

'Aye, Ed,' Knox replied. 'It's not a great connection, but carry on. I can hear you.'

'It's Fairbairn's blouse,' Murray said. 'The DNA results are in.'

'And?'

'A single hair was found on the garment. It came from a dog. Most likely an Alsatian.'

* * *

Knox and Fulton were crossing the Forth when his phone rang again. This time the caller was McCann, who told him Smeaton had been arrested without incident at Livingston. An ARV team were the first to arrive, but had not been required. Smeaton wasn't armed.

'They carried out a search of the house,' McCann told him. 'But no weapon was found.'

'Fine, Arlene,' Knox said. 'Where are you now?'

'Driving through Corstorphine,' McCann replied. 'Ten minutes from the nick. Smeaton's in the wagon behind us.'

'Has Mark been in touch?'

'Not yet. Last I heard he and Yvonne were parked up near Russell's office, waiting for another ARV team. HQ sent the first lot ahead of us, since you suspected the gun was Smeaton's.'

'Okay, Arlene, thanks,' Knox said. 'Bill and I are at South Queensferry. We'll see you at Gayfield Square in around twenty minutes.'

Chapter Twenty

When Hathaway relayed Knox's message to Naismith, the DCI contacted Gartcosh and asked to be put through to the Armed Response Control Unit. His call was taken by the duty officer, Superintendent Sean Grainger, who immediately despatched a stand-by team to Livingston, working on the premise that Smeaton was most likely to have the pistol.

Grainger told Naismith to instruct Hathaway to drive to Merchiston, but to keep Russell's premises under surveillance. No approach was to be made until the ARV team arrived. He advised Naismith that the second unit was being diverted from Shotts in west central Scotland.

Hathaway had followed this instruction, and he and Mason were parked at the foot of Merchiston Court awaiting the armed officers.

'Forty minutes now,' Hathaway said, glancing at his watch. He nodded to the door of Bluebird's premises, a short distance away. 'It's quiet,' he continued. 'I could take a wee wander up, make sure Russell's in his office.'

Mason gave him a determined look. 'You'll stay in the car,' she said firmly. 'You heard Naismith. They sent the first team to Livingston. Our lot should be here any minute.'

Hathaway shrugged. 'I just get peed off doing nothing, that's all.'

'Knox told you. We can't be sure which of the brothers has the weapon. You could get shot.' Mason shook her head. 'We'll wait until the ARV gets here. They'll handle it.'

Mason had just finished speaking when a black Range Rover turned into the street and stopped behind them. The driver's door opened and a burly-looking man in a dark uniform exited. He wore a peaked cap with a chequered band, and the epaulettes on his shoulders bore three chevrons.

Hathaway wound down his window as he approached.

'DC Hathaway and DC Mason?' the man inquired.

Hathaway nodded.

'I'm Sergeant Gordon Taylor, Armed Response. Where's number eleven? Russell's office?'

Hathaway motioned to the other end of the street. 'Three doors from the top on the left,' he said. 'We haven't seen any movement in the forty-five minutes we've been here.'

Taylor nodded. 'Okay. Here's how we're going to play it.' The sergeant pointed to the Bluebird Parcel Services office. 'We'll take the ARV and stop almost opposite the door. Our strategy will be to keep the entrance in view while using the vehicle for cover. You and DC Mason stay here until we give the all-clear – is that understood?'

'Yes,' Hathaway said.

Taylor got back into the Range Rover, reversed, then drove along the street and halted just short of the Bluebird office's entrance. He and his crew exited, went to the rear and took out their weapons – Heckler and Koch MP7 submachine pistols – then Taylor stood close to the Range Rover's offside wing and switched on a loudhailer.

The detectives heard Taylor's amplified voice call out: 'Russell! Armed police! Come to the door. Keep your hands in view.'

A long moment of silence followed, then Taylor repeated the order. Seeing no movement inside the premises, Taylor shouted a command, then he and two officers ran across the street and flanked the entrance. The fourth went to the rear of the Range Rover and took out a red-painted battering ram. Taylor and the others moved out from their positions and covered their colleague, who took only seconds to force open the door.

Taylor and his men entered, the sergeant repeating his imperative for a third time: 'Armed officers! Stay where you are and keep your hands in view!'

He and the others stormed inside, then a couple of minutes passed and Taylor emerged and beckoned to the detectives. Hathaway and Mason left the Vectra and went to the scene.

'We've checked the property,' Taylor said when they arrived. 'A one-room office and back room below, a two-room flat above. Both floors are clear.'

'Russell's done a bunk?' Hathaway said.

'Either that or he doesn't know we're after him yet,' Mason said.

Taylor was joined by his colleagues, then a Ford Transit entered the street and headed towards the office. Its driver, seeing the armed officers, drew to a standstill some twenty feet away.

Taylor and his men shouldered and aimed their weapons. The driver, a man in his early twenties, stared like a rabbit caught in the headlights, wide-eyed and ashen-faced.

'Keep your hands in view and exit the vehicle,' Taylor said. 'Slowly, so we can see your every move.'

The man complied, and Mason could see he was shaking.

'What's your name?' Taylor asked.

'T– Todd Mackenzie. I'm a driver with Bluebird Courier Services.'

'You work for Russell?' Taylor asked.

'With him, yes. I'm one of his contracted couriers.'

'Where is he?'

Mackenzie shook his head. 'Out on a delivery, I think.'

'Do you know when he'll be back?'

'No,' Mackenzie replied. 'When he phoned me earlier, he said he had a couple of deliveries to make. One in Abington, the other in Thornhill.'

'What time did he leave?'

'He called me about eleven this morning,' Mackenzie said. 'I think he was leaving then.'

'Why did he call you?'

'To let me know an urgent parcel had arrived for one of my clients. It's to be delivered this afternoon. Which is why I'm here.'

'Have you any ID?' Taylor asked.

Mackenzie pointed to the van. 'My driving licence. It's in my wallet in the glovebox.'

Taylor waved the muzzle of his weapon towards the van. 'Go and get it. Slow movements only.'

Mackenzie, still visibly nervous, complied. He opened the nearside door, flipped open the glovebox and took out a plastic wallet, which he proffered to Taylor.

Taylor nodded to his men, who went over and searched the van. The sergeant clicked on his weapon's safety catch, then glanced at Mackenzie's licence. 'What's your address?' he said.

'44 Chandler Street, Leith. I live there with my mum and dad.'

Taylor handed him back the licence, then one of the officers who'd examined the van gave a nod. 'Clear, Sarge.'

The sergeant turned to Hathaway and Mason. 'I'll let you talk to Mr Mackenzie,' he said. 'See if you can get a fix on Russell's exact whereabouts. I'll get onto HQ meantime and update them.'

As he and his team went back to the Range Rover, Hathaway gestured to the office. 'Would you care to come inside and speak to me and my colleague?'

Mackenzie glanced at the splintered doorframe. 'Okay,' he replied. 'Doesn't look as though I'll be needing a key, after all.'

'You have one?' Mason asked.

Mackenzie bent down and lifted up the corner of a rubber doormat, under which was a key. 'Not normally,' he replied. 'Russell said he'd leave it for me.'

Hathaway nodded to Taylor and his men, who were back in the ARV. 'Pity we hadn't known that a few minutes ago.'

They went into the office, then Mason said, 'You told us Russell was going to Dumfriesshire. Is that something he normally does? Drop off orders himself, I mean?'

'Yes,' Mackenzie replied. 'He makes a number of the firm's deliveries.'

'He has a van?' Hathaway asked.

'Uh-huh,' Mackenzie replied. 'He has a lock-up around the corner in Merchiston Mews. Keeps his van there.'

'What type of van does he drive?' Mason asked.

'Currently it's a Mercedes Sprinter, rented from Silverton Vehicle Hire. Usually it's a Ford Transit. He's not had the Transit long, though. It could be in for repair.'

'What colour is the Ford?'

'Dark-blue.'

'Which type of van did he drive before that?'

'Up to five weeks ago it was a VW Caddy. Ran it for a couple of years.'

Mason and Hathaway exchanged glances, then Mason said, 'You told us Russell had a couple of deliveries. One at Abington and the other at Thornhill. You're sure he had only the two?'

Mackenzie indicated the computer on the desk. 'You can check,' he said. 'He keeps all his current jobs filed under "Outgoing".'

Hathaway went to the other side of the desk and switched on the computer. The machine booted up and the screen blinked into life. The detective clicked on an icon entitled "Outgoing", then a spreadsheet opened. At the top of the document an entry read: AH Gently Pharmaceuticals, Abington. Tel 018642-3856476. 1 parcel/deliver 15 August, 2.45pm/status: out for delivery/courier: D. Russell.

Underneath this was a second entry, which read: Andrew Logan Engineering, Thornhill. Tel 018482-568456. 1 parcel/deliver 15 August, 3.45pm/status: out for delivery/courier: D. Russell.

Hathaway glanced at his watch and saw it was 2.55pm. 'These delivery times,' he asked Mackenzie. 'How accurate are they?'

'We try to deliver by the time stated,' Mackenzie replied. 'Russell's lost a few contracts due to late deliveries. He's insistent on keeping to schedule.'

Hathaway acknowledged this with a nod, then took his phone from his pocket and dialled the first number. A couple of seconds later, a woman's voice answered, 'AH Gently Pharmaceuticals. How can I help you?'

'Hi, I'm phoning to ask if you've received your parcel from Bluebird Courier Services yet. It was scheduled to arrive at 2.45pm,' Hathaway said.

The woman replied, 'Wait a moment and I'll check.' Hathaway held, and a few moments later she came back on the line. 'Hello?'

'Hello, yes,' Hathaway said.

'The package was delivered ten minutes ago.'

Hathaway thanked her, ended the call, then checked his watch again. 'Russell's just left Abington,' he told Mason. 'He's on his way to Thornhill.'

* * *

'I think you know why we've arrested you, Mr Smeaton,' Knox said. He and Fulton were sitting opposite the ex-paratrooper in the same room they had interviewed him a day earlier, and Naismith was again monitoring the exchange from the adjoining room.

'You understand the charge?' Knox continued. 'Aiding and abetting your brother, Donald Russell, who we suspect of carrying out two murders, one serious assault, and possession of a handgun, contrary to the Firearms Act of 1968.'

Smeaton nodded.

'You declined legal counsel? You know you're entitled to a solicitor, or to have one appointed for you?'

Smeaton shrugged. 'I lied,' he said. 'What's the point of denying it?'

'Okay,' Knox said. 'I'd like to go over several points we touched on the last time we spoke. You told us that after your brother was fostered at the Glenlee Care Home in 2002, you never saw him again, and that access was denied to you. Yet Mrs Grant, the woman who fostered him, told us it was you who declined to see him.'

'I was angry at the home for splitting us up,' Smeaton said. 'To be honest, I had a bit of a tantrum over it. I got into a fight with Mr Jenkins, the supervisor. I even trashed my room. The home thought it better if I didn't see my brother for a while after that. When Jack's foster parents got in touch a few months later, I was still angry. I decided I didn't want to speak to him again.'

'When did that change?'

'Soon after I came out of the army.' Smeaton shook his head. 'I was in Afghanistan. Helmand Province. A small village called Almalla. An IED went off about thirty feet in front of me. The two troopers nearest were literally blown apart; legs, arms, bloody pieces of kit flying everywhere.

'The incident happened only a month before I'd completed my stint and was due for demob. I was discharged with a severe case of post-traumatic stress disorder. I was in and out of God knows how many psychiatric units over the next six months.

'When I came to Edinburgh, I had a few jobs, but couldn't hold on to any of them. I was having so many bloody nightmares. It got so bad I was afraid of going to sleep.

'The only good thing in my life was Linda, who I met shortly before my final time abroad. She stood by me when I came out, saw me through the worst of the PTSD.'

'When did you see Jack again?' Knox asked.

'Three and a half years ago, at the beginning of 2015. I ran into a guy I'd known at the Glenlee Care Home. He told me he'd met Jack at a pub in Tollcross and they got talking. Turned out Jack had his own business. The guy told me what it was called, but I did nothing about it for a week or two.

'Linda and I were living in a real dump at the time. Two rooms, peeling wallpaper, no hot water. I was still in and out of work. Menial jobs; kitchen porter, brickie's labourer, that sort of thing. I decided for her sake it was time I got a grip, found something else. I remembered my brother and his business; thought he might be able to give me a job. I rang him, we met and he was delighted to see me. Gave me the start that turned my life around.'

'I thought he only took on self-employed drivers with their own transport?' Fulton said.

Smeaton nodded. 'He does. He bought me a second-hand van and gave me all the work I could handle. Over the next six months, I was able to repay the van and put a deposit on our house in Livingston.'

'Okay,' Knox said. 'I'd like to talk about the handgun. How you brought it into the country and, more importantly, where it is now.'

Smeaton studied Knox for a long moment, then said, 'After the IED incident I became paranoid. I became convinced ISIS was everywhere, watching my every move. Just waiting for an opportunity to finish the job.

'The prospect of going back to civvy street without protection terrified me. Soon after the IED attack, I persuaded the lance corporal in charge of armaments to register my pistol with a faulty recoil mechanism – a result of the blast. I got him to record it as returned. He issued me a new one, which I returned when I was demobbed.

'The first Glock I hid at the bottom of my kitbag in a box of smellies I'd received from Linda. I dumped the aftershaves and put the gun and a couple of ammo clips in the deodorant box just in case it was inspected. It wasn't. I was waved through customs.

'I kept the pistol on me during the first few months back in civvy street. Nobody noticed, and I was never challenged. When we moved to Livingston, I hid it and the clips in a hall cupboard.'

'But your brother knew you had the gun, didn't he?' Knox said. 'And at some point, you gave it to him. Or he took it.'

Smeaton shook his head. 'I made the mistake of telling him where I'd hidden it,' he said. 'Soon after I bought the house, I invited him to dinner. Afterward we'd had a few – Linda was in the kitchen at the time, she never knew about the pistol – and I told him about the sidearm and where I'd hidden it. It was only a couple of days ago I realised it was missing.'

'How did he get into the house?' Knox asked.

'He drove through on Monday. Waited until Linda left to do some shopping, then let himself in and took it.'

'He has a key?' Knox said.

'I keep a spare under a plant pot near the door. I made the mistake of telling him that, too,' Smeaton replied.

'So, when you spoke to us yesterday, you knew Donald had shot McGeevor?'

Smeaton nodded. 'Yes.'

'You also knew he'd murdered Connie Fairbairn?'

'Yes.'

'He'd admitted it?'

'Yes.' Smeaton shrugged. 'It began back when I started working with him three years ago. When I told him about my PTSD nightmares, he became interested, told me he suffered from nightmares, too. More, he said there were times when he felt he was being possessed. Said he heard voices. Later, six months or so back, he told me that he'd been experiencing unusual urges.'

'What kind of urges?' Knox asked.

'Like he wanted to kill somebody.'

'Uh-huh,' Knox said. 'Go on.'

'I said he should seek professional help. I told him I'd seen any number of shrinks with my PTSD. That latterly I'd found them helpful.'

'But he didn't see anyone, did he?'

'No.'

'He told you he had an urge to kill,' Knox said. 'When did you suspect he'd acted on it? That he'd committed the Longniddry murder?'

'When I heard the Broxburn van dealer had been shot.'

'You tackled him about it?' Knox asked.

'Uh-huh,' Smeaton replied. 'I rang him on Monday afternoon and arranged to meet him at the office. He apologised for taking the pistol, then told me about a girl he'd almost strangled about a month ago in his VW Caddy. He said he'd traded it in with McGeevor, who had promised to sell it on to a dealer in Newcastle. He feared you might be able to trace it and charge him with attempted murder.

'He told me he traded it for the Transit and all seemed okay at first. Then McGeevor rang him at the weekend; he hinted that if he didn't pay an extra £1,000, he would contact the police.'

'He told you McGeevor attempted to blackmail him?'

'Yes, he told me he panicked. Said he knew if McGeevor did that–' Smeaton hesitated. 'It was then he told me about the Fairbairn girl. How they'd driven down the coast. He said he never intended her harm; he was only interested in sex. He didn't remember killing her, just that he had some sort of black out. When he came to, she was dead.'

'He believed McGeevor suspected him of the killing?' Fulton said.

Smeaton nodded. 'Apparently McGeevor said as much when he phoned. Don took the gun to Broxburn with the intention of frightening him. But then they argued, and he shot him.'

'You were with him when he torched the van?' Knox asked.

'Yes. He thought there might be DNA somewhere. He asked me to help him get rid of it.'

'You never thought of the possibility he might turn on you?'

Smeaton shook his head. 'Never,' he said emphatically. 'Maybe because of our childhood trauma, maybe because we both have psychological troubles, and maybe because we're flesh and blood.' He shook his head again. 'No, I never felt that.'

'The pistol,' Knox said. 'What happened to it?'

'Don told me that when he left McGeevor's place he wiped it down with an oily rag, stuck it in a plastic bag, and chucked it down a drain.'

'You believe him?'

Smeaton shrugged. 'He was anxious to get rid of the Transit. I reasoned he'd be equally anxious to get rid of the gun.'

* * *

'Hathaway's just been in touch from Merchiston,' Naismith was saying. Smeaton had been escorted back to his cell and Knox and Fulton had joined the DCI in his office a few minutes later. 'One of Russell's couriers turned up at the office. He gave Hathaway Russell's delivery schedule. He just dropped off a parcel in Abington and is currently on his way to make a second delivery in Thornhill.'

'You've set up an intercept?' Knox asked.

Naismith nodded. 'Aye, I've asked Dumfries and Galloway Police to collar him and take him to Dumfries nick. We'll head down there now and pick him up.'

'I take it they've an ARV unit with them?'

'I'm not sure, Jack. Why?'

'I think there's a strong possibility Russell might still be armed.'

Chapter Twenty-one

The driver told them he was headed for Carlisle, and dropped them off at the Leadhills Road junction of the A74 and B797. When he drew to a halt, he gestured to the junction and glanced at his watch. 'Almost half past two, girls,' he said. 'You shouldn't have long to wait until someone stops and gives you a lift. I hope you enjoy your visit to Drumlanrig Castle.'

Weber and Fischer thanked him and crossed to Leadhills Road, walking a short distance to a straight stretch where they took up position and stuck out their thumbs.

The first few vehicles, mainly cars, drove on; then a white Mercedes van slowed and came to a stop.

When Fischer approached the passenger door, the driver, a good-looking man in his late twenties, wound down the window.

'We're going to Drumlanrig Castle,' she told him. 'It's near Thornhill?'

'Okay,' the man said. 'Jump in.' As the girls settled into the passenger seats, he asked, 'Where are you from?'

'Germany,' Fischer replied. 'Stuttgart.'

The man nodded. 'I thought you had a bit of an accent,' he said. 'What are your names?'

'I'm Imke,' she replied. 'My friend's name is Lena.'

He checked his door mirror and pulled away. 'My name's John,' he replied. 'John Masters.'

* * *

Naismith had notified Dumfries and Galloway Police of the likelihood that Russell was armed and the inspector who took the call advised that an ARV team had been alerted. It was on its way to Thornhill where it would join local officers.

The DCI, Knox and McCann had been on the road for thirty-five minutes, and were passing through Biggar with Fulton and Herkiss following in the Corsa.

'I asked Hathaway and Mason to stay put at Russell's office,' Knox said. 'Taylor, the sergeant in charge of the ARV team, is going to remain in place, too. In case Russell gets back early.'

'But Hathaway phoned the pharmaceutical company at 2.45pm,' Naismith said. 'Russell's got another delivery in Thornhill. You think he might not follow through?'

Knox shook his head. 'I honestly don't know, Alan,' he said. 'Russell lied to his brother about the circumstances of McGeevor's murder. He claimed it was the result of an argument, when in fact ballistics has suggested it was premeditated. He's unstable and unpredictable. I just want to make sure we're covering all the bases.'

* * *

'I'm not that much of a sci-fi fan myself,' Russell was saying. Weber and Fischer had told him about their fascination with the *Outlander* series and that they were going to Drumlanrig because an episode had been filmed there.

'You haven't seen it?' Fischer asked.

'I don't watch much television. My sister-in-law does, though. I've heard her mention it,' Russell said.

'You're not married?' Fischer asked.

'No,' Russell replied. He glanced over, first at Fischer, then at Weber. He didn't think much of the brunette, but the blonde sitting next to him was a real beauty. She had high cheekbones, a pert, dimpled chin, and cobalt-blue eyes. She wore her hair plaited in the German style at either side of her head, and there was no doubt in his mind that the colour was natural.

He'd have preferred if the blonde had been on her own, and had hesitated for a moment before picking them up.

Still, there might be a way that could be resolved…

'I could take you all the way to Drumlanrig if you like,' he said, then nodded to the rear of the van. 'I've only one more parcel to deliver in Thornhill. It's only a short distance farther on. If you'd wait till I drop it off.'

Weber smiled. He was gratified to see she had perfect teeth, too.

'You wouldn't mind?' she said.

He grinned. 'Mind? Of course not. Actually, the castle's a wee bit off the A76. Three or four miles. It would save you a walk.'

Weber smiled again. 'That is really very kind of you.'

'Yes,' Fischer agreed. 'We would be happy to stay with you until you deliver your parcel.'

Good, Russell thought. An idea of how to separate them had formed in his mind. Andrew Logan Engineering's premises was located off the A76 a mile the other side of Thornhill. It was a squat, red-brick building on one level at the foot of a steep, single-track road. There was enough room to turn the van in the car park, which was where he'd put his plan into action.

He had now left the B797 and joined the A76, and the women were still babbling excitedly about Drumlanrig and the two central characters in the *Outlander* series, Claire Randall and Jamie Fraser.

'It is such a beautiful country, Scotland,' Weber said. 'The mountains, the lochs, and the castles.'

'Yes,' Fischer agreed. 'Many things look as they must have been during Jacobean times.' She turned to Russell. 'Do you not think so, John?'

He'd never been all that interested in the past. All that mattered to him was the here and now. But he went along with their enthusiasm.

'Yes, the country is pretty much unspoilt. As you say, nothing much has changed in centuries,' he said.

A few minutes later, he gestured at the windscreen. 'Here we are, girls. Thornhill. The place I'm delivering to is just up ahead.'

He carried on for a couple of miles, then indicated left and turned onto the narrow track leading to Logan's premises.

The road was flanked by tall hedgerows on either side and, after negotiating a sharp bend halfway down, he arrived at the car park, which was just wide enough to enable him to execute a three-point turn.

He came to a stop with the van facing the exit, then leaned over to Fischer and smiled. 'Imke,' he said, 'would you do me a favour?'

Fischer eyed him curiously. 'A favour?'

He reached behind the driver's seat and took out a small leather satchel, opened it, and removed a card-covered notebook. 'This is my last drop of the day,' he said. 'I'm required by law to make a record of delivery times and the van's mileage.' He nodded to Logan's entrance. 'It's just a small parcel. Would you take it to the desk and give it to the receptionist?' He took a pen from his shirt pocket and indicated the journal. 'Meanwhile I can update my logbook. It'll save time. We can be on our way to Drumlanrig sooner.'

Fischer nodded. 'Okay.'

'Good,' he said.

Fischer exited the van and waited until he came around and slid open the side door. He took out a small cardboard box, handed it to her, then motioned to the building. 'Thanks, Imke,' he said. 'Just hand it over. It doesn't need a signature.'

Fischer began walking towards the building. Russell slid back the door and waited until she'd entered, then dashed back around and got inside.

He started the engine and put the van into gear.

'What are you doing?' Weber said, a look of alarm on her face. As the vehicle edged forward, she added, 'No! Wait for Imke.'

'We're going without her, sweetheart.'

When Weber turned to the door, Russell put a hand into the satchel, took out the Glock, and pressed it into her side. 'Try that, sweetheart, and I swear I'll shoot you.'

Weber glanced at the gun, then shook her head. 'Why are you doing this?' she asked.

'Never mind,' Russell said. 'Just do as I tell you, understand?'

Weber bit her lip. 'Yes,' she replied.

Russell placed the pistol on his lap, then drove back up the hill. He had almost reached the top when a police patrol car turned into the road, blocking his escape.

His face clouded with anger as he was forced to stop, then the officer at the passenger side exited the car. He pointed to Russell and shouted, 'Out of the van.'

Russell wound down the window, then grabbed the Glock and fired twice. The first shot shattered the car's nearside headlamp, and the second caught the officer in the shoulder.

The patrolman staggered back inside the car, then the driver rapidly backed up the hill, reversing into the road leading to the A76.

Russell drove to the junction. Seeing his exit to the main road blocked by the patrol car, he turned left onto the B2370. A couple of miles farther on, he rounded a bend and saw another police car straddling the road a short distance ahead.

Russell slowed, checked his mirror, and saw the strobing blue light of a second police vehicle at his rear. He was weighing up the chances of ramming the patrol car ahead when it was joined by a police Land Rover.

His eyes scanned for a way out, then he saw a sign fifty yards ahead, which read: 'FARM COTTAGE TO RENT'.

He turned onto the track and drove a short distance, coming to a halt at a gate behind which was a red-brick cottage. He motioned to Weber and said, 'Out!'

The girl did as he asked, standing immobile as he walked around the van and grabbed her arm. Russell led her to the door of the cottage and tried the handle, but found it was locked.

He let Weber go, waving the muzzle of the pistol in her face. 'Don't make a move,' he said.

He stuck the Glock in his waistband, took a couple of paces back, then thrust his shoulder at the door. He repeated the action twice more, then the jamb splintered and the door gave way. Russell retrieved the gun and pointed it at his hostage. 'Inside,' he said. 'You and I are going to be here till I sort things out.'

* * *

Knox and the others were passing through Carronbridge on the A76 when Naismith's phone rang. The caller was the Dumfries and Galloway officer the DCI had spoken to earlier, DI Stewart Campbell.

'I'm sorry, sir,' Campbell said. 'But Russell's managed to escape.'

'What happened?' Naismith asked.

'I had three men posted inside Logan Engineering's premises,' Campbell replied. 'I asked them to make sure no cars were visible at the front of the building. The idea was to wait until Russell entered the premises and we'd collar him at reception. But he sent in a girl.'

'A girl?'

'Yes. A German tourist by the name of Imke Fischer. She and her friend were hitch-hiking to Thornhill with the intention of visiting Drumlanrig Castle. Russell picked them up near Abington.'

'What happened to her friend?'

'I was coming to that, sir,' Campbell said. 'After Fischer went in with the parcel, Russell took off with her. The moment my officers realised what was happening, they radioed their colleagues. A patrol car tried to block Russell's van on the narrow road leading to Logan's premises. He took a shot at one officer, who was wounded. The driver backed out of the way, but managed to stop him rejoining the A76. Russell turned into the B2370, where two of our vehicles were waiting. When Russell saw them, he turned off the road.'

'Where is he now?'

'He forced his way into an empty farm cottage,' Campbell replied. 'My men have the place surrounded.'

'Is the ARV team there, too?' Naismith asked.

'Only just arrived, sir. It came all the way from Annan.'

'You're at the scene?'

'Yes, sir.'

Knox keyed in the B2370 coordinates into his Passat's sat nav, then turned to Naismith. 'We're about six miles away, Alan.'

The DCI nodded, then spoke into his phone. 'Okay, Stewart,' he said. 'We'll be with you in ten minutes.'

Chapter Twenty-two

When they arrived at the scene, Knox saw five police vehicles and a dozen or so officers clustered around the start of a short, rutted track.

Russell's van was parked at a gate at the end. A small yard was located to the left of the cottage, at the edge of which stood a barn that was partially obscured by trees.

Campbell introduced the others, among whom was a four-man armed response team headed by a tall sergeant called McCarthy.

'Have you tried to contact Russell yet?' Naismith asked Campbell after the DI affected introductions.

'No,' Campbell replied. 'We've the owner's landline number, but the phone's disconnected.'

Knox took out his mobile, scrolled through its contacts list, then pressed *call*. A moment later Hathaway answered, 'Yes, boss?'

'Is Mackenzie still with you?' Knox asked.

'Yes, boss. I detained him in case Russell got back in touch.'

'Good, Mark. Get Russell's mobile number off him, will you? Text it to me ASAP.'

'Okay, boss.'

Knox ended the call and turned to Campbell. 'Are any of your team trained in hostage negotiation?'

Campbell shook his head. 'Dave Cosgrove's the only one at Dumfries who's completed the course. He's currently on another job.'

Knox acknowledged this with a nod, then his phone beeped as Hathaway's text arrived. He turned to Naismith, who shrugged. 'You speak to him, Jack,' the DCI said. 'We can't wait until Cosgrove's dragged off whatever case he's on and brought here.'

Knox keyed in the number and a moment later Russell answered, 'Yeah?'

'Don?' Knox said.

'Who's that?' Russell sounded edgy, ill-at-ease.

'Detective Inspector Jack Knox. We spoke at Merchiston.' He paused. 'You've got a young woman with you? Lena Weber?'

'I have,' Russell replied. A moment's silence, then, 'I've got a gun, too. A Glock 17. Plus two spare clips.'

'Yes, I know. I spoke to your brother.'

'Ryan said I'd a gun? I told him I'd got rid of it.'

'He wasn't sure if you had or not,' Knox said. 'Look, Don, Ryan's only concerned for your welfare.' A pause, then, 'Why don't you give yourself up?'

'Oh, aye,' Russell said mockingly. 'And spend the rest of my life in Saughton?' There was a moment's silence, then he added, 'Or Carstairs? Maybe you think I'm some kind of nutjob?' A short pause, then he continued, 'Give myself up? Not bloody likely. Your lot had better bugger off and allow me free passage out of here. You know what'll happen if you don't.'

'We can't do that, Don,' Knox said. 'Come on, son. Let the girl go. She's done you no harm.'

Knox heard Russell give a snort of derision. 'She's done me no harm, I agree,' he said, 'but I swear I'll do her some. A fucking bullet in the head, if you don't do as I say.' He said nothing for a long moment, then added, 'I'm switching this phone off now. You've five minutes, then I'm coming out. The bitch will have the Glock's muzzle pressed to her throat and my finger on the trigger. I want clear passage back to the A76 and no tails – on the road or in the air. If I see a cop anywhere near, I'll let her have it.'

Knox had his mobile switched to speaker mode and the others had heard the conversation. As he ended the call, Naismith said, 'We can't bargain with him.'

Knox shook his head. 'No, Alan, we can't. There's a real chance he'll kill her.'

Sergeant McCarthy, the senior armed response officer, addressed Naismith. 'The roof of that barn gives clear sight of the cottage,' he said. 'More, the approach is obscured by trees.' He nodded to one of his men who, like himself, was clad in black fatigues. The man was in his mid-thirties, slightly-built, with close-cropped hair. 'Rory Gifford's my best marksman,' he added. 'With your permission, sir, I'd like to go to the barn and help him onto the roof. He'll be armed with a Heckler and Koch G3, rifle and sight.'

'You think Gifford can take him out?' Naismith asked.

McCarthy nodded. 'Yes, sir. No question.'

'You understand Russell will have the Glock at her neck?' Knox said.

'I do, sir,' McCarthy replied. 'All Gifford needs is for him to take the muzzle away for a fraction of a second. Then he'll act.'

Knox turned to Naismith, who nodded. 'There's no other way, Jack,' he said.

'Okay,' Knox said, then to McCarthy, 'Do you have a megaphone?'

'Yes,' McCarthy replied, pointing to the Range Rover. 'There's one in the ARV.'

'Good,' Knox said. 'I'll wait till Gifford's in place then tell Russell we're agreeing to his demands. We'll move the vehicles back out of sight of the track. Radio me when you're in position. But, sergeant…'

'Sir?'

'Tell Gifford to take the shot only if he's sure he can get Russell without risking the hostage.'

'Sir.'

McCarthy went to the Range Rover and removed a megaphone, which he gave to Knox; then he and Gifford took their weapons and moved cautiously along the path, taking care to keep to the trees and out of sight of the farmhouse.

A few moments later they arrived at the rear of the barn. Gifford slung the rifle over his shoulder, then McCarthy cupped his hands and gave his colleague a leg-up. Once Gifford had elbowed his way into position on the sloping roof, the sergeant radioed Knox.

'We're in place,' he said. 'Gifford's got a clear line of sight to the cottage door.'

'Okay,' Knox replied. 'We've moved the cars. Tell Gifford to get ready. I'm about to give Russell a shout.'

The radio crackled in response. 'Sir,' McCarthy replied.

Knox switched on the megaphone and called out: 'Russell! This is Knox speaking. We've moved away from the entrance and you've clear access to the A76. You can come out now. But remember... no harm must come to the girl.'

The radio crackled into life again. McCarthy said, 'He's coming out with the hostage.'

McCarthy relayed this information from the corner of the barn, then dodged back out of sight. As he moved, the heel of his boot caught a length of dry twig, which snapped with a resounding *crack*. His colleague, meanwhile, had the G3 sighted on Russell's forehead.

What happened next was over in seconds.

When he heard the snap, Russell flinched, then took the pistol from Weber's throat and swung it in the direction of the barn.

Gifford chose that exact moment to trigger the rifle. The high-velocity round ripped into Russell's head just above his right eye, throwing him back through the doorway.

Weber screamed and ran to the gate. 'Target hit,' McCarthy said over the radio. 'I repeat, Russell is down and the hostage is making her way towards you now.'

* * *

McCann and Herkiss drove Weber back to Logan Engineering, where they picked up Fischer and returned both girls back to Edinburgh. There, Weber was treated for a mild case of shock and the women's statements were taken. Naismith arranged transport back to the airport, where the companions boarded a flight back to Stuttgart.

'Mr Andrew Logan, boss of Logan Engineering, offered the girls a return trip for early next year,' McCann told Knox. 'He's offered to pay for flights, accommodation, transport and admittance to Drumlanrig Castle.'

'Nice gesture,' Knox said.

'It was,' McCann agreed. 'The girls were delighted, despite their ordeal.'

The detectives were assembled in the Major Incident Inquiry Room, and a few moments later Naismith left his office and joined them. 'I've just taken a call from the Chief Constable,' he said. 'The media have been quite fulsome in their praise, and of course he's delighted with the outcome. He's asked me to extend my congratulations to you all.'

He turned to Mason and added, 'You'll be pleased to hear, Yvonne, that the Procurator Fiscal won't be taking further action on the stop by Traffic officers at Abbeyhill. What's more, Chief Superintendent Mullin's upheld my charge against Reilly for insubordination and attempting to bring the reputation of a fellow officer into disrepute. Reilly has been knocked back two grades to Detective Constable and suspended from duty for six months.'

Mason gave a sigh of relief. 'Thank you, Alan,' she said.

'You're welcome, Yvonne,' Naismith said.

The DCI rubbed his hands together, looked at Knox, and then Herkiss and McCann. 'The Chief's called us back to Gartcosh, Jack. Effective immediately. Warburton's been advised he can return and take up his post here again tomorrow morning.' He grinned. 'Your fiefdom is all yours again.'

Knox extended his hand. 'It's been a pleasure working with you and your colleagues, Alan.'

Fulton, Hathaway and Mason chimed their agreement, then Naismith said, 'With the exception of Reilly, eh?'

'There are always exceptions,' Knox said.

* * *

After the Gartcosh officers had left, Knox said goodnight to Fulton and Hathaway, then went over to Mason. 'We never did get around to celebrating my birthday properly, did we?' he said.

'You mean because I had to get up early?'

'Yes. You were up before I was.'

'I was, wasn't I?'

'You think we should do something about it?'

'You've still got some Absolut?'

'The bottle's almost a half-full.'

'Mmm,' Mason said. 'I'd better leave my car here.'

'You'd better.'

'Because you don't want to tempt fate?'

'Uh-huh,' Knox said. 'I think I've got all the temptation I can handle.'

The End

List of characters

Officers based in Edinburgh:

Detective Inspector Jack Knox – head of the Major Incident Inquiry team based at Gayfield Square Police Station, Edinburgh

Detective Sergeant Bill Fulton – Knox's partner, second member of the Major Inquiry Team

Detective Constable Yvonne Mason – third member of the Major Inquiry Team

Detective Constable Mark Hathaway – fourth member of the Major Inquiry Team

Detective Chief Inspector Ronald Warburton – senior detective at Gayfield Square Police Station

Detective Inspector Edward (Ed) Murray – forensics officer with the Scottish Police Authority (SPA)

Detective Sergeant Elizabeth (Liz) Beattie – forensics officer and Murray's assistant

Sergeant Cox – bereavement counselling officer based at St Leonard's Police Station, Edinburgh

Gartcosh team:

Detective Chief Inspector Alan Naismith – officer in charge
Detective Inspector Charles Reilly
Detective Sergeant Gary Herkiss
Detective Sergeant Arlene McCann

Other officers:

Detective Sergeant Bob Lightfoot – photofit specialist
Detective Chief Inspector Ross Miller – liaison officer
Chief Superintendent Mullin – chair of tribunal
Chief Superintendent Dave Ramsey – tribunal officer
Chief Superintendent Nigel McCrone – tribunal officer
Chief Inspector Brian Forsyth – officer representing Mason
Detective Chief Inspector George Laidlaw – officer representing Reilly
Superintendent Sean Grainger – Armed Response Control officer
Sergeant Gordon Taylor – head of armed response team at Merchiston
Detective Inspector Stewart Campbell – Dumfries and Galloway control officer
Sergeant McCarthy – head of armed response team at Thornhill
Police Constable Rory Gifford – marksman on McCarthy's team
Detective Inspector Quinn – investigating officer with the Broxburn office
Police Constable Cullen – officer with DI Quinn at Broxburn

Detective Inspector June Short – ballistics forensic specialist

Detective Inspector Brian Fraser – ballistics forensic specialist

Detective Inspector Dave Keller – officer at Penicuik police station

Sergeant Byers – Traffic officer

Police Constable Lyall – Traffic officer

Others:

Alexander Turley – pathologist

Peter Taylor – Longniddry resident who discovers Connie Fairbairn's body

Connie Fairbairn – murdered girl

Mrs Ellen Fairbairn – murdered girl's mother

John Masters – pseudonym used by the killer

Shona Kirkbride – Connie Fairbairn's friend

Joe Turner – a man Masters meets at the Quaich pub, Grassmarket

Glenn Carnegie – Radio Forth news announcer

Roy Duttine – assistant manager at Bungo's

Evie Lorimer – girl Masters picked up at Doonan's pub

George Lawton – owner of Jackson's Garage and stockist of Byrona tyres

Jackie Lyon – Central Lowland Television's senior news reporter

Donald Russell – owner of Bluebird Parcel Services

Walter Coates – independent courier

Lee Spence – independent courier

Willie McGeevor – used van dealer based in Broxburn

Scott Reynolds – McGeevor's business partner

Shafiq Khan – Bluebird courier

Maureen Somerville – Bluebird courier
Deborah Horsefall – Bluebird courier
Derek Norton – Bluebird courier
Mrs Norton – Derek's wife
Jeff Norton – Derek's son
Ryan Smeaton – Bluebird courier
Linda Smeaton – Ryan's wife
Todd Mackenzie – Bluebird courier
Bernie Mackenzie – Todd's father
Mrs Mackenzie – Todd's mother
Archie and Elsie Grant – Master's foster parents
Lena Weber – German tourist
Imke Fischer – German tourist

If you enjoyed this book, please let others know by leaving a quick review on Amazon. Also, if you spot anything untoward in the paperback, get in touch. We strive for the best quality and appreciate reader feedback.

editor@thebookfolks.com

www.thebookfolks.com

MORE FICTION BY ROBERT McNEILL

Available on Kindle and in paperback:

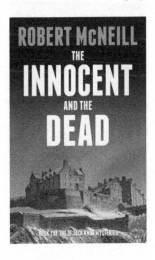

The Innocent and the Dead

Book 1 of the DI Jack Knox mysteries

One girl is found dead – strangled in the woods. Another, the daughter of a rich, well-connected businessman, is kidnapped. Unassuming detective Jack Knox must solve these two cases. But the Edinburgh crime-solver will have a hard time getting his superiors to accept his unconventional methods. Will he gamble too much?

Dead of Night

Book 3 of the DI Jack Knox mysteries

When a philandering French college lecturer is killed and
unceremoniously dumped in a canal, DI Jack Knox soon
discovers there is no shortage of spurned lovers and
jealous husbands who might have done it. He sets about
collaring the culprit, but will his efforts be thwarted by
unfair complaints made about the investigation?